Montgomery Lake High #5
The Forces Within

Written by Stacy A. Padula
Edited by Michael Mattes

Briley & Baxter Publications | Plymouth, Massachusetts

Paperback ISBN: 978-1-7350168-8-7
Hardcover ISBN: 978-1-7331536-9-0

Book Design: Stacy O'Halloran

Dedicated to Max Alva

Meet the Characters

Top: Andy, Chantal, Cathy, Jon
Middle: Katherine, Lisa, Leslie
Bottom: Bobby, Jeff, Chris

Learn more about the characters at www.stacyapadula.com

Follow them on Instagram:
Cathy @ckagelli99
Chantal @chantal_kagelli
Lisa @lisa_ankerman99
Chris @dunkin_85

Part I
When Lightning Strikes

"And He said to them, 'I saw Satan fall like lightning from heaven. Behold, I give you the authority to trample on serpents and scorpions, and over all the power of the enemy, and nothing shall by any means hurt you. Nevertheless do not rejoice in this, that the spirits are subject to you, but rather rejoice because your names are written in heaven.'" – Luke 10:18-20

PROLOGUE

<u>Andy Rosetti</u>

I'm going to come right out and be blatantly honest with you; this story is probably going to confuse you to no end. I still cannot fully comprehend what happened to me or discern reality from illusion. I catch myself wondering if I am even awake or if I am even alive. Is this all just a dream? How can I tell? What happened to the people I remember loving? What about the few people I highly disliked? Have they melted together?

Twice in the past month, I have woken up in a world that I cannot recognize. At first, everything seemed somewhat normal, but then I began hearing things that didn't align with my memories. Just when I had begun to accept the world I first woke up in as my life, I was thrown for a loop. I woke up in a completely different world with a completely different set of emotions. Somewhere along the line, I have lost my identity, my sense of reasoning, and my personality.

I have been trying my best to write off the first world as a dream within a dream, because that has seemed most logical. I would love to do that and continue living contently in the second world that I woke up in; I just can't. There are too many strange coincidences between the two worlds. There are too many surreal things happening for me to allow myself to accept this life as my own. In my head, I know who I am, how I am supposed to feel, the moral code I live by, and how the people I am close to behave. Unfortunately, all of that exists only in my head and certainly not in this life (I think) I live in.

CHAPTER 1

Chantal Kagelli gripped her boyfriend Andy Rosetti's hand tightly and shook off a chill. She planted her eyes on Leslie Lucus, who was leading their pack of friends into the woods. They had ventured out of Leslie's lake house, in search of the abandoned foundation that Leslie had mentioned during their three-hour drive from Montgomery.

"So, where exactly are we going?" Jon Anderson asked from in front of Chantal. He was walking beside Katherine Rossi and holding her hand.

"It's awfully dark out here," Katherine said. "And cold," she added as she leaned in closer to Jon.

"It's only a little further," Leslie assured them as she shined her flashlight on the narrow path that they were traveling. "It's just past that clearing up ahead." Leslie was walking arm in arm with Lisa Ankerman. Bobby Ryan was on the other side of Lisa.

Chantal assumed that the sight of Jon and Katherine—together—was causing Bobby a significant amount of pain. *What an odd mix of people*, Chantal thought. *Andy and Jon on the same vacation? Katherine, Jon, and Bobby spending a weekend under the same roof?*

"Does your family own this land, Leslie?" Chantal asked.

"Uh, my parents don't, but I, uh, know it pretty well," Leslie stammered.

She sounds nervous, Chantal thought.

"Don't worry, Chantal. People are not going to mind if we cut through their woods," Jon said and turned around to face her. Jon's words brought Chantal no comfort. How could he possibly comfort her while holding Katherine's hand? She sighed and leaned closer into Andy's body. He squeezed her hand tightly.

Just as they approached the clearing—which was actually a pond with a narrow path around it—the sound of a roaring engine echoed through the air. Chantal jumped, momentarily losing her grip on Andy's hand. Headlights appeared in the distance and illuminated their surroundings. Chantal noticed a bridge to her left that appeared to lead into a thick forest. She turned back toward the headlights and squinted.

"Hey!" a man's angry voice sounded through the air. "Get out of my woods!"

"Oh, crap!" Leslie cried out. "That guy's crazy!"

Chantal set her horror-stricken eyes on the oncoming vehicle.

"Go, go, go!" Jon screamed as he fled across the bridge and disappeared into the thickly brushed woods to the left of the path. Every part of Chantal wanted to run after him, but she could not move her limbs.

"You can't run from me, you little punks!" the man hollered out of the truck's window.

"Come-on! Come-on! Run! Run!" Andy cried. He stole Chantal's hand and darted after Jon into the woods. "Get on your hands and knees! You have to crawl through this!"

"God help me!" Chantal heaved in panic as she heard the truck's door slam shut. She dropped to her hands and knees.

"You can't go anywhere! You're on an island!" the man yelled.

"Move, move, move!" Bobby, who was crawling behind Chantal, demanded.

"He's right behind me!" Katherine shrieked. "Jon!"

"I'm sick of you delinquents trespassing on my property. You just wait 'til I get my hands on you!" the man yelled into the woods.

"I can't get through this!" Chantal cried. She closed her eyes and dropped to her stomach as Andy pulled her under a broken tree branch.

"Shhh! Shhh!" Jon hushed from up ahead.

With only the haze covered crescent moon illuminating the blackness of night, Chantal and her friends scrambled further into the heart of the island.

"You're on an island!" the man hollered, sounding closer to them with each syllable. "Where do you think you're running?"

Reaching a less thickly wooded area, Chantal and Andy rose to their feet. Nearly hyperventilating, they dove into a ditch that was surrounded with briars and brush. Chantal landed hard on her knees and winced in pain. The "ditch" was actually the broken-up foundation that Leslie had previously mentioned.

Andy lay on his stomach, a few feet beside Chantal. "Shhh," he hushed.

Chantal's ears caught the sound of crackling brush. A moment later, Andy rose to his feet and peered over the foundation's wall.

"Who is that?" Chantal whispered to him.

Andy shrugged and raised a finger to his lips. Squatting back down beside Chantal, he tightly squeezed her shaky hand. The woods seemed to become unnaturally silent. Warily, Andy rose and pushed himself up and out of the foundation. "Grab my hands," he hissed, extending both of his arms in Chantal's direction. "Hurry and be quiet."

Chantal nodded and took his hands into her sweaty palms. Pushing her feet against the concrete wall, Chantal used the aid of Andy's pulling to climb out of the five-foot foundation. Standing up beside Andy, she observed her still surroundings. She heard a car door slam shut in the distance. Glancing around, Chantal could not locate any of her friends.

Andy took Chantal's hand and led her further into the woods. "Hey," he hissed, looking right and left. Everything remained still.

"Did the guy leave?" Chantal asked as she proceeded quietly behind Andy.

"Maybe, but he sounded awfully pissed," Andy replied. "I wouldn't be surprised if he had a gun. I mean, that guy went sick."

"Andy, he could rape me!" Chantal cried.

"Shhh!" Andy hushed and halted abruptly.

"What?" Chantal questioned him as she began darting her eyes in all directions.

"Run!" Andy shouted as he forcefully grabbed Chantal's hand.

Off to their immediate right, an engine roared. Headlights shone from behind Chantal and Andy as they dashed around trees and sprinted through briar patches. The infuriated maniac had gunned his truck straight into the woods, knocking down everything in its path to the old foundation.

Tears streamed down Chantal's face and blood dribbled down her legs as she bolted through the woods. The distinct sound of a branch snapping caused Chantal to halt in her tracks. She glanced around for the source of the sound. Suddenly, a dark figure jumped in front of Andy and struck him across the forehead with a tree branch.

Andy fell to the ground, while Chantal let out a chilling scream that echoed throughout the night's air. She stood frozen in fear over Andy's unconscious body.

The dark figure stepped over Andy's lifeless body and advanced toward Chantal.

Chantal stood paralyzed—defenseless. As the figure moved closer, Chantal collapsed to the ground.

The figure knelt down in front of her and lifted her chin.

Panicked, Chantal jumped back and lost her balance. Flustered and uncoordinated, she pushed herself to her feet.

"Chantal?" the dark figure asked. The voice she heard belonged to Jon.

Chantal froze, staring with distrust at the person in front of her. *Why would Jon attack Andy?* Chantal took one step back from the person.

"Chantal, it's me," Jon said and stepped closer to her. He placed a hand on her shivering shoulder.

"Jon, why did you hit Andy?" Chantal questioned him accusingly.

"That was Andy?!" Jon exclaimed and immediately dropped to the ground where Andy lay unconscious. "I thought it was the guy taking you captive!"

"We were running because that guy drove into the woods after us," Chantal explained and knelt beside Jon. "We ran for a few minutes, but I'm sure he's still searching for us. We have to get Andy out of here."

"Okay, we have to move fast and quietly," Jon said as he attempted to lift Andy's body off of the ground. "I really thought that guy had caught you."

"Can you carry him?" Chantal asked as she tried to help Jon lift Andy.

"I got him," Jon replied and rose to his feet. "All right, go. Hold all the big brush aside for me to get through, okay?"

"Where are we going?" Chantal asked as she carefully stepped over a fallen tree branch. "You can't carry him forever."

"We have to get away from that lunatic and find the water around this island," Jon whispered to her.

"At least the trees aren't as close together here as they were where we entered the island," Chantal commented as she hustled down a makeshift path. "It almost seems like we're on a path."

"Hopefully, it will lead us to the shore," Jon said with a sigh.

The sound of a door slamming in the distance made the hairs on Chantal's arms stand up straight. "I hope he didn't find anyone," Chantal said and turned around to face Jon. Her eyes spied a shadow lurking not too far behind him. Halting in her tracks, Chantal gasped.

"What?" Jon questioned her.

Two dark figures began running toward them.

"Hey!" Jon called out. "Who are you?"

The people continued running toward him and Chantal.

"Jon?" Leslie asked from within a five-foot distance.

"Oh, thank you, Lord," Chantal sighed and finally caught her breath. "Oh, it's Bobby, too. Good, he can help carry Andy!"

"I'm so glad to find you guys! I lost my flashlight running from that guy, and it is so dark in these woods! Luckily, I ran into Bobby. It's good you guys were together," Leslie rambled. "I know a place where we can go to get away from this nut. We have to keep moving, though, because I heard him say something about calling the cops. What happened to Andy? Why is he unconscious?"

"We'll explain later. Just lead us out of here," Jon replied tensely. "Bobby, give me a hand with him."

Picking up their paces, the group soon reached a clearing. The moonlight above illuminated a dirt road ahead. "Where will that take us?" Chantal asked as she ran beside Leslie toward the road.

"There, uh, is an abandoned house not too far from here. It's nice—not haunted or anything. It should be pretty clean too because the owners just moved out over the summer," Leslie replied. She slowed her pace as she reached the road.

"So, we could stay the night?" Chantal inferred.

"My dad's driving up tomorrow afternoon, so as long as we're back to my cottage by then," Leslie said with a shrug.

"I hope that guy isn't waiting at the house," Jon said as he and Bobby caught up with the girls—they were at either end of Andy's body.

"Don't even say that," Chantal said as she glanced uneasily at Jon.

"Hey, we'll do what we can to protect you girls, but I'm not making any promises," he teased her.

"Jon, that's not even funny!" Chantal scolded him and placed her arms across her chest. "You have a good point, though. I mean that guy must know the house is the only place we can go."

"That's not very comforting," Bobby remarked. "Hopefully, Kat and Lis are there already."

"Why would they be there?" Leslie questioned him with a strange twist in her usually warm tone.

Bobby shrugged. "I just hope they're okay," he said.

"I cannot believe you guys left Katherine!" Chantal exclaimed disapprovingly.

"We'll go look for her and Lis after we settle in the house," Jon stated flatly. "There's nothing more we can do now."

"We really should just hurry up and keep our voices down," Bobby said.

Chantal and her friends made their way to the end of the dirt road, at which point it merged with a concrete driveway. Tall willow trees lined the driveway, covering it like a hood and blocking all traces of the moonlight.

Further down the driveway, the trees parted, and the haze-covered moon illuminated the walk. Up ahead, the shadowy outline of a Victorian home came into Chantal's sight. It did not appear old or rundown, and even the yard seemed recently landscaped. Verandahs and balconies wrapped around both sides of the house, and a detailed stairway led up to an inviting front porch.

"Leslie, are you sure no one lives here?" Chantal asked as she hesitantly followed her friends up the stone walkway.

"Yes, Chantal, I am *sure,*" Leslie stressed.

"Don't jump down her throat or anything, Lee," Jon stated sarcastically. "I think Chantal has more than a right to ask that question. In fact, she was the one hesitant about the woods in the first place. Maybe if we had heard her out, we wouldn't be in this situation."

"Oh, ya think?" Leslie snapped at Jon as she climbed the grand front steps.

"Lee, open both doors so we can get Andy inside more easily," Bobby said. He followed Jon through the French doors and into the darkness of the entranceway.

CHAPTER 2

Andy stared at Chantal, trying to process the last few words she had spoken. Her words were not registering in his mind, as if she had been speaking a foreign language. *How long was I unconscious? This doesn't make any sense,* he thought.

"Leslie found the light switch. This room is right off of the foyer. Jon and Bobby laid you on the couch and then went back outside to look for Lisa and Katherine," Chantal continued to explain. Her green eyes were full of concern as she spoke.

"So, all of this just happened ten minutes ago?" Andy asked as he tore his eyes off of Chantal's pretty face. Even with leaves and twigs tangled in her long auburn hair, Chantal still looked like the most beautiful girl in the world.

"Well, in the last half hour. You were unconscious for almost twenty minutes," Chantal clarified and took hold of his hand.

"Anderson did this to me?" Andy questioned her as he gently touched his forehead with his other hand. *I hate that kid.*

Chantal sighed. "It was a mistake," she said and turned away from him.

"No, he just wanted time alone with you," Andy reasoned out loud. *Everyone knows he still loves you.*

Chantal pulled her hand away from his. "Jon and I are a thing of the past," she said sternly. "He's going out with Katherine now, anyway. You have no reason to worry about his intentions."

"What?" Andy asked. *This has to be a dream.* "Jon's going out with Kat? What happened to Jon and Julianna? Bobby and Kat are together. They have been a couple for a year." Andy peered at Chantal, for once thinking his levelheaded girlfriend might be a little crazy.

"No, Andy. Katherine and Bobby broke up last month," Chantal said slowly. She raised her eyebrows at him expectantly. "Remember?"

"I swear, I had no idea," Andy said, feeling more confused than ever. *If Bobby and Katherine are no longer a couple, then this has to be an alternate world.*

In silence, Bobby trudged across the clearing and into the woods with Jon. Jon was the last person Bobby wanted to spend time with. Armed with the flashlight he had taken from the mansion's butler closet, Bobby peered into the thick woods to his right. Jon was a few feet in front of him, shining his flashlight into the woods on the left. They were on the path that had led them to the mansion.

The woods seemed to grow thicker and darker with each passing moment. The air felt thick—in an eerie way—which made Bobby feel like the trees were closing in on him. Although he knew it was an illusion, he could not shake the chill that had crept up his spine.

"This island is huge," Jon said as he paused to push aside a tree branch. "I'm trying to find the water."

"Maybe this path will lead us back to the bridge," Bobby said.

"There it is!" Jon exclaimed.

Bobby hustled over to Jon and glanced through the trees. He saw the reflection of Jon's flashlight shining on the water.

"Hopefully, that dude isn't parked on the bridge," Jon said.

"If this path even leads to the bridge," Bobby stated dryly.

Without warning, Jon took off running.

"Where are you going?" Bobby called out. Wasting no time, he ran after Jon. With his flashlight shining on Jon's back, Bobby watched him halt suddenly.

"What the heck?!" Jon shouted.

Bobby stopped short beside Jon and glanced down at the fifteen-foot, eighty-five-degree drop to the water. "Where's the bridge?" Bobby asked, struggling to bring his voice above a whisper.

"There was a bridge here," Jon stated. "I know this is where we entered the island." He shined his flashlight across the water.

"I don't know how you can be so sure," Bobby said. "We were frantic when we crossed the bridge. I didn't know what was around me or where I was headed."

"Look, the shore is only about ten feet from here, and it just gets further away to our left and right," Jon said.

"Dude, there was no path when we crossed the bridge, just thick woods," Bobby said. "That much I can remember."

"Right, but then that crazy guy drove his truck into the woods and knocked down some of the trees," Jon stated earnestly. "Look at the water! I think I see part of the bridge floating over there."

"No freakin' way," Bobby said, hoping that Jon was as delusional as he was arrogant. "There is no way that guy could've knocked down the bridge."

"It looks that way though, doesn't it?" Jon asked as he moved the beam of his flashlight from one floating wooden board to another.

"You have *got* to be kidding me!" Bobby exclaimed, as he realized that Jon's theory was true. "Swimming back to Leslie's cottage? That'll be flippin' awesome."

"She better know another way out of here," Jon said and turned away from the water. "Let's just keep looking for the girls. Once we're all together, we can figure out a plan."

Bobby sighed and followed Jon deeper into the woods. "Katherine? Lisa? Hello?" he called loudly. The woods were silent, apart from their own footsteps. *I just hope the girls are together, wherever they are,* he thought. *How could I have let Katherine out of my sight?*

Jon stopped short, causing Bobby to stumble into him.

"Geez, Lis, you almost gave me a heart attack! Why didn't you answer us?" Jon exclaimed.

Bobby looked over Jon's shoulder to see Lisa, sitting between two trees, one yard in front of him. Bobby sighed with relief.

"Sorry, but you can never be too sure in situations like this," Lisa replied. "Everyone scattered in a hundred directions, and then that crazy guy destroyed the bridge. I knew you guys would find me if I stayed in one place."

Jon sat down on a tree stump beside Lisa.

"Where's Katherine? She's not with you?" Bobby asked. Vibes of panic rushed through his body.

"Um, I know she's tiny, but she's not invisible," Lisa said and rolled her eyes.

"Well, everyone else is back at a house that Leslie took us to. We all met up, except for you and Katherine," Jon explained.

"Then we should go to the house and organize a search party for Kat," Lisa said. She began brushing dirt off of her jeans as she stood up. "How do we get there?"

"There's a path," Jon replied.

"Lis, when you saw that guy leave the island, did he have anyone with him?" Bobby asked.

"Oh, no, no. He was completely alone. You weren't thinking that he got Kat were you? Oh, no. No way," Lisa replied and followed Jon over a fallen tree.

"Then she must be in these woods," Bobby reasoned out loud. *She must be so scared,* he thought. *Why doesn't Jon seem as worried as I am?* "I am staying out here until we find her. There is no way she is spending the night out here alone."

"At least one of you sounds worried about her," Lisa remarked dryly and nudged Jon.

"Hey, I'm just as worried as anyone else," Jon stated defensively. "I just don't know what else to do."

"There's no way you're as worried as I am," Bobby said as he tried to fight off the urge to tackle Jon to the ground. *It would feel so good to punch you across the face.* "You do not have a fraction of the feelings that I have for Katherine. You're too self-centered to love anyone but yourself." *Go ahead and punch me, Anderson.*

Jon paused and then turned around to face Bobby. "You have no right to insult me for dating your ex-girlfriend. If you love her so much, then why didn't you keep track of her?"

"Oh, that's right! You don't insult your ex-girlfriend's boyfriend; you just hit him over the head with a tree branch," Bobby retorted.

"Cut the crap, guys!" Lisa shrieked as she stepped between Bobby and Jon. "What is happening here? We all want to find Kat, agreed? Why does it matter who wants to find her more? This competition is not helping the situation, by any means. Maybe I'm more worried about her than either of you are. Who knows? Who cares? Let's just find her!"

Bobby remained silent, staring eye-to-eye with Jon.

"Let's go!" Lisa demanded and pushed Jon in the shoulder. "Lead me out of these woods."

Jon took a deep breath and turned away from Bobby. "All right, let's go," he said sternly.

Reluctantly, Bobby followed Jon and Lisa. Going back to the house and organizing a search party was a logical plan, but Bobby really did not want to leave Katherine alone in the woods. "Katherine!" he called out as loudly as he could. No matter how many times he yelled her name, he always got the same response: silence.

Chapter 3

Chantal followed Andy up the mansion's grand, richly carpeted front staircase. "It doesn't make sense that no one lives in this *gorgeous* house!" she exclaimed. Dangling within the two-story foyer, the oversized crystal chandelier illuminated the second-floor hallway above. Chantal ran her fingertips along the dustless cherry railing, wondering who was in charge of the mansion's upkeep. Except for the foyer, where Chantal and her friends' muddy shoes were piled, each room that she entered appeared spotless.

"You said that Leslie went to lock the doors and windows?" Andy asked as he paused on a landing in the staircase.

"Yeah, that's what she said," Chantal replied and halted at Andy's side. She glanced up at the twin staircases that stemmed from the landing. "Which way should we go?"

Andy took Chantal's hand and stepped onto the staircase to his left. "This way," he said. "Leslie?" he called out loudly. "Are you up there?"

"She could still be downstairs," Chantal whispered as a chill shot up her spine.

"Just stay right here for a second, okay? I'm going to check the hallway at the top of the stairs," Andy said and tightly squeezed Chantal's hand before making his way up the remaining stairs.

Watching Andy disappear into the darkness of the second-floor hallway, Chantal felt eerily alone, as if Andy would never return. The thought of losing him in the mansion was enough motivation to send her charging up the staircase after him. She turned down the dimly lit second-floor hallway and rushed up behind her boyfriend. "Hey!" she shouted as she playfully bumped into him.

Andy jumped.

"I'm sorry! Did I scare you?" she apologized and threw her arms around him. "I just would rather be by your side than alone."

Andy sighed. "It's okay."

"So, what's down these halls?" Chantal asked curiously. "They don't seem *too* long."

Andy shrugged. "I doubt Leslie's up here, so we might as well go back downstairs," he said and turned back toward the stairs.

"Well, what's up those stairs over there?" Chantal questioned him as she peered down the hallway in front of her.

"Just another hallway I'm sure," Andy replied, thumping down the stairs toward the foyer. "We can check out this place more when we find everyone."

"*If* we find everyone," Chantal stated warily as she turned toward the stairs to follow Andy.

"Hun, I know there are a lot of places you'd rather be—and I'm sure you'd rather be with different people, too—but we have to make the best of this," Andy said as he paused on the landing and waited for Chantal to reach him. "I know Leslie, Kat, and Lis aren't your best friends, but they like you, and maybe this trip will bring you guys closer together."

"Maybe," Chantal replied halfheartedly as she stepped ahead of Andy down the grand set of stairs. "It's just funny that people who 'like me' treat me so rudely sometimes."

"Who was rude to you?" Andy asked as he jumped off the last step onto the foyer's marble tile.

Chantal sighed as she spotted Leslie coming around the corner. "Oh, speaking of the devil," she said quietly. She couldn't help but notice the way Leslie's face lit up at the sight of Andy.

"Hi, guys!" Leslie greeted them warmly as she entered the foyer. "Oh, Andy, how are you feeling? That is *awful* what Jon did to you. To think he mistook you for that psycho! Almost unimaginable, huh? Well, at least you know that he had Chantal's best interest at heart."

"Excuse me?" Chantal asked. "My best interest is far from seeing Andy hurt."

"Oh, you know that's not what I meant," Leslie retorted. "All I meant was that it's *good* that you and Jon are so... close," she added and glanced at Andy.

Andy let out a heavy breath and smiled. *He looks upset*, Chantal thought as she observed his expression. Slowly, he glanced over at Chantal. She turned away from him and glared at Leslie. *Pressing one of the only issues that causes tension in our relationship is far from coincidental*, Chantal reasoned. She wished that Andy could see how callous Leslie truly was.

Chantal jumped as the front door swung open with great force. "Get inside!" Jon screamed as he lunged into the foyer. "I've had enough!"

"*You've* had enough?" Bobby asked with a laugh. "You—Mr. I'm-too-into-myself-to-give-a-*crap*-about-anyone-else—are sick of me? *You* stole my girlfriend from me. *You* took Katherine; the only person I have ever loved—the girl I centered my life around for over a year! But you're my friend, right? Okay, 'friend,' take the person who matters most out of your life and realize that they've vanished, knowing that if maybe you had done one thing differently, they could be safe in your arms. Try that on for size, Anderson."

Jon dropped his brown eyes to the floor. Deep scarlet washed over his face as he stalked past Chantal and up the maroon-carpeted staircase.

Bobby shook his head as he pushed past Lisa. He slammed the heavy mahogany door as he exited the house.

"Lisa, are you okay?" Leslie asked and rushed toward her.

"Oh, me? I'm fine," Lisa replied. She crossed her arms and stared blankly ahead. "Kat, on the other hand, I just don't know about," she stammered. She shook her head as her green eyes filled with tears. "We searched those woods," she added quietly. "Katherine is gone."

"Oh, come-on, Lis," Andy sang, moving away from Chantal to Lisa's side. "She has to be out there somewhere; we're on an island!"

"An island, Andy? No," Lisa said and shook her head. "You can believe what you're supposed to believe, what you've been tricked into believing. Or you can find the truth. Right now, I'm going to find a warm bed to sleep in. And Leslie? Stay the hell away from me."

Chantal watched Leslie's jaw drop as Lisa stormed up the staircase. *Odd,* she thought. *Lisa rarely shows emotion.* She glanced at Andy. He had lowered his eyebrows and was staring strangely at Leslie. "I wish I knew what she meant by that," Andy muttered.

"Me, too," Leslie said and smiled awkwardly. "I hope she's not blaming this on me just because my cottage is a mile from here."

"Well, Leslie, I'll give you this," Chantal said. "You did a great job locking the front door."

"What?" Leslie questioned her defensively.

"Maybe next time you should try turning the lock, so more of your friends don't disappear," Chantal suggested. She held her cold gaze on Leslie before running up the stairs after Lisa.

CHAPTER 4

After Chantal rushed upstairs, Leslie and Andy remained in the foyer. "Is everything my fault?" Leslie asked as she threw her arms out toward Andy. "I mean, I invited you guys here. If I hadn't done that, then Katherine would be safe, Jon and Bobby wouldn't be in a fight, Lisa wouldn't be pissed at me, and Chantal wouldn't be mad at you," Leslie ranted.

"*What* are you talking about?" Andy questioned her with skepticism. "Chantal's not mad at me."

"Come on," Leslie sang dramatically and raised her eyebrows. "You don't really think she's only angry with me, do you? As far as Chantal is concerned, *you* led her into this situation. Because of you, she's trapped on an *island,* away from everything comforting to her. On top of that, she had to aid you back to health."

"No, you don't know Chantal," Andy said and shook his head. "She doesn't see things that way."

"Well, then she's lucky that you're here," Leslie said and put her head down. "To tell you the truth, I wish Adam were here to reassure me that everything will be all right. At least he wouldn't blame me for this mess."

"Leslie, I don't think you're at fault here. This isn't about who's at fault," Andy assured her and placed his hand on her shoulder. "This is about making the right decisions in a stressful situation."

Leslie nodded. "You're right. I'm being self-centered."

"Lee, I didn't say that," Andy stated and shook his head. "What I meant—"

"—No, it's okay," Leslie interrupted him and stared directly into his eyes. "Now, I know how to handle this." Slowly, she stepped toward him.

Staring back into her sea-green eyes, Andy fought the temptation to cave into her pleading gaze. *I know she wants me,* he thought. *She wants me, and she is dating my friend.* Inching closer to him by the second, Leslie threw her arms around Andy. Andy hesitantly stepped toward her. A vivid picture of Chantal flashed across Andy's mind, and he immediately tore himself out of Leslie's arms.

Hustling across the foyer and up the staircase, Andy scolded himself for being so defenseless against Leslie's seductive manner. Frantically scurrying up the left staircase, Andy desperately glanced in all directions for Chantal. To his disadvantage, he knew nothing about the mansion's floor plan. To his right was an old-fashioned sitting room—vacant, as expected. Two doors were down the hallway to his left, three were to his right, and the staircase that Chantal had pointed out was straight ahead of him.

Shutting off the hall light, Andy observed light shining from beneath one of the doors to his left. Knowing that he'd either find Jon, Lisa, or Chantal through that door, Andy paused for only a second before barging in. To his surprise, the room was empty—except for two twin beds and an antique dresser. Across from the doorway, a set of glass doors led to a balcony. Two doors lined the wall to Andy's left, one slightly ajar. Traveling across the carpeted room, Andy made his way toward the ajar door and squeaked it open. As he did, two sets of startled eyes met with his.

Andy felt the color on his face drain, as his heart dropped to his stomach.

Having made way to the bedroom of her choice—the one that she had always slept in—Lisa gazed aimlessly up at the stars through the glass doors. Her chosen bedroom was to the right of the main stairs, where guests hardly ventured—although, Lisa was more like a returning occupant than a guest.

Keeping her eyes on the stars as she crept across the hardwood floor, Lisa stepped onto the balcony that wrapped around much of the mansion. Before, it had seemed to go on forever, but now, its ending nearly slapped her in the face. *It's funny how life's misfortunes can change one's whole perspective,* she thought.

Leaning against the wrought-iron railing, Lisa glanced below to the abandoned courtyard. The courtyard was much like her: chipping apart. It had once been an appreciated childhood spot, but now, the stone was cold. A single tear streamed down Lisa's cheek—one that she felt no need to wipe away. Crying meant emotion, which, most of the time, Lisa dared not to show. That moment was different, though; her life was flashing clearly before her eyes. Most other times, she wouldn't allow herself to live a moment with such honesty and clarity.

"Lis?" a voice called out from her left. Unnoticed, the French doors off the servants' hall had opened onto the balcony. Andy stepped outside with his arms crossed and his head down.

Frantically wiping the tears from her face, Lisa turned away from her best friend and leaned far over the railing.

"Lisa," Andy said as he walked over to her. "I want to know the truth."

Still staring at the ground below, Lisa showed no recognition of Andy's presence.

"Lisa," Andy repeated with his voice sounding edgy. "Don't pull this crap with me! What the heck is going on?!"

Lisa sighed and turned to make eye contact with Andy. "I don't want to talk. I just want to be alone," she muttered.

CHAPTER 5

Staring at Lisa on the balcony, Andy sensed her sadness. He knew that he was the only person to ever see that side of Lisa—the side her fake front didn't mask. Andy knew Lisa better than he knew anyone, even Chantal. Andy had been there for Lisa through the most trying times of her life, and it pained him to see her in such a broken state. After all that she had been through in the past couple of years, it was remarkable that she hadn't completely collapsed. Through it all— even her father's death—Lisa had felt comfortable confiding in Andy. If she couldn't talk to him under these circumstances, then there had to be a lot more to the situation than Andy was aware. He stood on the balcony and held his gaze on her, refusing to move an inch away.

"Andy, I just want to be alone," Lisa stated firmly and pushed herself up on the railing. "I'm fine. Really."

"No, you're not," Andy said and shook his head as he jumped up beside her. "There is something bothering you, and that bothers *me*."

"It bothers *you?*" Lisa questioned him with a short laugh. "I think you have a lot of other things that should be bothering you right now," she said and failed to meet Andy's eyes. "I mean, you have a bruise on your forehead that is painful to speak about. Chantal suspects that you're cheating on her with Leslie, and I know that you want to. I know it bothers you to see Chantal close with Jon because of your own semi-guilty conscience. And you know what else?"

Ouch. "You might as well lay it on me," Andy replied. He swallowed the large lump in his throat and stared intently at Lisa.

"Jon doesn't like Katherine, and Chantal still owns his heart," Lisa said with a sympathetic look in her green eyes. "You know that she's been questioning your relationship, lately, and it's pretty obvious that she compares you with Jon. But all of this you know and just won't admit to yourself."

"Oh, really?" Andy questioned her and crossed his arms uncomfortably.

"You know friendship goes both ways, Rosetti," Lisa said with a laugh. "I don't always have to be the one with the story, and I shouldn't be the only one who's honest. You've got to talk to me because I know you have problems, too."

"I'm glad you noticed," Andy said sarcastically.

"Seeing that I'm usually high, it's surprising how much I notice," Lisa joked and nudged him playfully.

"True," Andy agreed and spread his lips into a small smile. "This whole situation has been explained to me, but something doesn't feel right. You and Leslie are keeping something from the rest of us— something about Katherine and this island, this house and that psycho-guy."

"Really Andy, it's nothing," Lisa assured him as she glanced down at her fingernails. "Leslie just pisses me off sometimes. That's all."

"Don't lie," Andy said. "I know you better than anyone. I understand that you don't want to talk about it right now, but don't say that there is nothing wrong when I know there is. Stop lying to yourself; it's only going to cause you more pain."

Lisa remained silent and turned away from Andy.

"But you're right about me being in denial," Andy added as he jumped down from the railing. "I guess I'm kind of like you; I tend to put up a front that my life is perfect. Even Chantal thinks my life is perfect."

"Nobody's that lucky," Lisa commented dryly and smiled awkwardly.

Mirroring her smile, Andy turned away from her, toward the open French doors. "Oh, Lis?" he called before entering her bedroom.

"Yeah, buddy?" Lisa replied from atop the railing. She was staring blankly at the courtyard below.

"It's my turn to talk tomorrow, all right?" Andy called to her and smiled warmly.

"Yeah, all right, Rosetti," Lisa replied and smiled back. "I'm going to call it a night, too, I guess," she added and jumped off the railing. "Where are you crashing?"

Andy shrugged. "I was hoping to share a room with Bobby or Chantal, but I don't see that happening. When I came upstairs, Chantal and Jon were talking in a bedroom. They'll probably crash in there together. It's funny how she'll never sleep in the same room as me."

"That's because she knows what you'll try," Lisa teased him and sent a playful smirk in his direction.

"Well, I don't see *that* happening any time soon."

"Hey, that's her decision and you gotta respect it."

"Oh, I do. I just—"

"—Goodnight, Andy," Lisa said, cutting him off. She laughed as she fell back onto her turned-down bed.

"Night, Lis," Andy said and shut the door behind him as he crept into the shadowy hall.

Up ahead, where the foyer's light diminished, a door creaked. Andy halted in his tracks. His heart pounded against his chest as the creaking door slammed into its frame. Although part of him wanted to turn down the main stairs and find a cozy bed—preferably near Chantal's—the majority of him wanted to investigate the mysterious sound. Lightly stepping down the carpeted hallway, Andy ran his fingers across the wall, in search of a light switch. Walking past the glass-pained doors that led onto the balcony, he remained in darkness. Tensing his muscles as he reached the far end of the hall, Andy took a deep breath. There was only one other door aside from Lisa's and the balcony's off of the narrow hallway. It was the door that had slammed—the door Andy stood facing. He let out a heavy breath.

Clueless about the mansion's floor plan, Andy reminded himself of the limitless possibilities of where the door could lead. Lightly pressing his ear against the door, the sound of running water twitched his eardrum. Dropping to his knees, Andy peered beneath the door for any sign of light. Oddly, whatever was behind the door appeared to be in a state of complete darkness. He eyed the door suspiciously and weighed his options. *It has to be one of my friends running the water. Doors don't just slam by themselves! Whoever slammed the door was obviously seeking attention—probably Leslie.*

Andy tapped his knuckles softly on the wooden door. He received no response. Once again, he knocked—much harder this time. Still, the only sound that met his ears was the continuous running water. He paused for a moment and gazed oddly at the door in thought. *It would be rude to just barge into someone's room, and it would be embarrassing to disrupt someone's shower. But who showers in the dark?*

Turning the brass doorknob, Andy slowly creaked the door open. After he opened it halfway, he saw no sign of life. Stepping into the darkness, Andy quietly shut the door behind him. Searching the wall to his right, he flicked on a light switch, illuminating the large room: a kitchen/den combo with white cloths covering various pieces of furniture. The walls were painted the muted color of mayonnaise, and the rug beneath Andy's sock-covered feet was faded beige. Moonlight shone through six windows—three of which overlooked the balcony. Lining the wall to his left were three pine doors and a narrow staircase.

Andy crept across the carpet to the only open door. Resting in the doorframe, he observed the tiny bedroom before his eyes. While flicking a light switch, he stepped into the room. Its decor was the same as the kitchen's, but the walls were windowless. The twin bed against the far wall had been turned down. Upon the plush comforter rested a set of keys and a thick wad of money. Why any of his friends would carry around so much money failed to register in Andy's mind. Studying the set of unfamiliar keys, he contemplated over whom they might belong to. As a stomach-turning thought entered his mind, the splattering of running water became obsolete. *What if the person in the shower is not one of my friends?*

Andy stood frozen, deep in contemplation. Without a clue as to who was in the bathroom, he fled across the room to the closet's slender door. As the bathroom door creaked open, Andy stepped silently into the closet. Leaving only his fear-filled eyes uncovered, he layered himself with clothing.

Attempting to breathe silently, Andy listened intently to the noise coming from outside the closet. Despite how thin the carpet had seemed, it succeeded in muffling any possible footsteps. Pushing himself deeper into the closet's corner, he eyed the door expectantly, envisioning the psycho from the woods that Chantal had described.

Sweat clothed Andy's body. Curling his legs to his chest, Andy breathed deeply.

Slowly the brass doorknob began turning. Light illuminated the closet as the door creaked further and further from its frame. Horror stricken, Andy wrenched his eyes off the floor. Hesitantly raising his chin, Andy set his eyes upon the intruder. Leaning against the doorframe and staring aimlessly ahead was Leslie, engulfed in a plush white towel.

CHAPTER 6

***

Chantal yawned and extended her arms high over her head. As she wrenched her eyes open, Jon came into focus. He was standing across the room, pulling a navy-blue polo shirt over his head.

"Morning, beautiful," he greeted her with a smirk as he adjusted his collar.

Chantal sat up straight and uncomfortably darted her eyes around the room. Reflecting on the previous night's events, Chantal gazed questioningly from Jon to the messy lump of sheets beside her.

"What's wrong?" Jon questioned her with apparent amusement. "You look surprised to see me."

Chantal rose from the bed and smiled at him awkwardly. Glancing down, she felt a sense of relief wash over her as she made note of the wrinkle-less jeans and sweater that covered her body. Walking past Jon, whose eyes had remained plastered upon her, Chantal studied her reflection in the nearby cherry-framed mirror.

"You look great," Jon said from beside her.

Still holding her gaze in the mirror, she eyed Jon's reflection skeptically and tried to discern his motives. "Thanks," she replied, watching her cheeks grow red in the mirror.

"So, why don't we go find everyone else?" Jon suggested and lightly tugged on Chantal's messy auburn ponytail.

"Yeah, why don't we?" Chantal agreed and fixed her hair into a loose bun. "Then, I can explain to Andy how I didn't intentionally sleep next to you."

"If that's the truth," Jon said facetiously and opened the bedroom door.

Chantal rolled her eyes and sighed as she walked past Jon into the adjoining bedroom.

"Chantal, I slept in this room," Jon stated with a laugh. "You fell asleep mid-sentence, so I left you alone. I would never disrespect you like that."

Chantal turned around and smiled at Jon before exiting the bedroom.

That morning, Andy paused in the kitchen before descending into the breakfast room where Lisa and Leslie were conversing. Lisa's tone caused Andy to stop in his tracks. Curiously, he strained to make out the tense words that were being spoken in the next room.

"Leslie, this is getting ridiculous," Lisa said. "We have to find Kat and get out of here."

"No!" Leslie cried. Her voice was much louder than Lisa's and easier for Andy to understand.

"This isn't fun!" Lisa exclaimed. "*No one* is worth spending another day in this house."

Who? Andy wondered. *Katherine?*

"Whatever," Leslie said.

"You are so selfish," Lisa stated flatly.

She sounds so irritated, Andy thought. His thoughts were broken by the sound of heavy footsteps coming toward him. "Hey!" he cried, stepping into the breakfast room as Lisa breezed past him without a greeting.

"Hi," Leslie replied half-heartedly, without glancing up at him. Her eyes were locked on her breakfast.

"That's some pretty interesting cereal you got there," Andy said and sat down at the cherry table beside her. "I'm surprised the kitchen had food."

Leslie remained silent and moved the dry corn flakes around in her bowl.

"So, where'd you end up sleeping last night?" Andy asked nonchalantly.

Leslie shrugged. "Some room upstairs. Why, where were you last night?"

"Some room upstairs," Andy replied and smiled slightly.

"Hi," Bobby mumbled as he entered the room. His expression was just as dreary as the weather outside the bay window.

"Hey, where'd you go last night?" Andy questioned him while studying the dark circles under his eyes.

Bobby shrugged and sat down across from Leslie. "For a walk," he replied lifelessly.

"Later, we have to look for Kat," Leslie stated. "We'll find her, Bob. Don't worry."

At the sound of Leslie's words, Bobby immediately rose from the table and stormed out of the room, nearly colliding with Jon and Chantal. Chantal entered the room behind Jon. After making her way to the table, she sat down across from Andy.

"Good morning, Chantal," Andy greeted her. "Did you sleep well last night?"

Chantal glared at him. "I'm sure more soundly than you did," she replied in a hard-to-read tone.

Andy felt the color drain from his face. She was looking at him as if she knew he had slept in Leslie's closet.

"We passed Lis on the stairs. What's her deal?" Jon asked from beside Chantal.

Leslie shrugged. "Drug withdrawal?" she suggested in a sarcastic tone.

Andy rolled his eyes. "That, I doubt."

"So, Katherine hasn't turned up?" Jon asked and sent questioning glances at Andy and Leslie.

"No," Leslie replied and shook her head. "We'll look for her in a little while."

"Oh, yeah! I forgot! *Katherine's* the girl you're dating," Andy exclaimed and rose from the table. "Some vacation," he added before stalking out of the room. He hustled up the stairs and then turned right at the landing, rushing toward Lisa's bedroom.

"Lis?" he called and tapped lightly on her bedroom door.

"Yeah?" Lisa replied.

"It's Andy. Are you okay?" he responded and opened her door. "Hey, Lis."

"Hey, buddy," Lisa replied down-heartedly and motioned for him to sit beside her on the bed. "What's up?"

"What's up with you?" Andy questioned her with concern.

"What? Did Leslie tell you that we got in a fight or something?" Lisa asked dryly.

"Well, I kind of got the message when you breezed past me without any sort of greeting," Andy replied. "Then Anderson, who I'd like to punch, noticed something was up with you, too."

"Why do you want to punch Jon?" Lisa asked while she reached into her pocketbook.

"Because I think he's trying to hook up with Chantal. They both seemed uncomfortable at breakfast, and for all I know, something could have happened last night," Andy explained. "I don't think Chantal would ever cheat on me, but she can be a flirt."

"Where'd *you* end up sleeping last night?" Lisa asked as she pulled a small bag of marijuana and papers out of her pocketbook.

"Truthfully?" Andy asked and raised his eyebrows with hesitation.

"Uh, huh," Lisa said as she broke up a pinch of the drug onto a paper.

"In Leslie's closet," Andy replied, trying to sound as nonchalant as possible.

"What!" Lisa exclaimed, looking up at him with intrigue-filled eyes.

"Promise you won't say anything to anybody?" Andy asked.

"Promise," Lisa pledged.

"When I left your room last night, I heard a noise down the hall, so I checked it out," Andy said, debating how detailed to make the story.

"Let's go outside," Lisa suggested and gestured toward the balcony.

"Anyway," Andy said and rose from the bed to follow Lisa onto the balcony. "I found my way into a servant's bedroom. I was wicked confused as to why anyone would stay in there. Then I heard someone coming, so I hid in the closet."

"You dork!" Lisa teased him. She smiled as she perched herself up onto the balcony's railing and lit her joint. "So, how'd you know it was Leslie's room?"

"Because she came in the closet," Andy replied.

"Did she see you?" Lisa questioned him with curiosity and amusement written all over her attractive face.

Andy shrugged. "I *definitely* saw her."

"Did anything happen?" Lisa pressed him. She hesitated slightly before offering him the joint.

Andy shrugged and hesitantly took the joint from her fingers. *What am I doing?* he thought. *I don't want to get high. I'm confused enough already.*

"Get high, and you'll tell me," Lisa said.

"I shouldn't even be doing this," Andy stated. He took a small hit off the joint before handing it back to her. He had forgotten how much he hated the taste of marijuana and the way it burned his lungs. "Getting high is against all my morals."

"You're a funny kid, Rosetti," Lisa commented and rolled her eyes.

"I'm messed up, that's what I am," Andy said. "My life is the biggest contradiction, seriously. After the most uncomfortable night's sleep, I had to face Leslie *and* Chantal this morning at breakfast."

"How did she not see you?" Lisa asked and again passed Andy the joint.

"I don't know," Andy replied. "But it was one crazy experience," he added after taking a second hit from the joint. His body began to feel light, and he remembered why he enjoyed smoking weed.

"She saw you Andy! She must have!" Lisa exclaimed. "I bet she intentionally lured you into her room. She wants you to like her. She told me the other day that the whole reason for this trip is so she can hook up with you."

"What? No way. Are you serious, Lisa?" Andy questioned her. "Then why did she invite Chantal?" The disappointment in his tone alarmed him. He took another hit off the joint before passing it back to Lisa.

"You would cheat on her, wouldn't you?" Lisa inferred.

"No, I love her. I'm just getting baked, so leave me alone," Andy replied. "Lis, look at what you did to me! A piece of dental floss could probably blindfold my eyes! I'm not supposed to smoke up; I'm Class President. I can't be doing this crap with you anymore."

Lisa shrugged. "At least you know Leslie wants you."

"For a virgin she seems awfully eager," Andy stated bluntly.

"Well, some girls, like Chantal, think of their virginity as a gift to cherish and protect. Then there are girls, who surrendered it a long time ago. There are also girls, like Leslie, who want to have sex but can't because their boyfriends believe in waiting," Lisa explained.

"So, is that what's been going on between you and Leslie? She's been saying all this is worth it because she wants to hook up with me?" Andy questioned her.

"There's a lot more to it than that," Lisa replied and dropped her eyes to the ground.

With her arms folded across her chest, Chantal sat upon an antique Victorian sofa in the dimly lit, second-floor sitting room. She ignored the faint footsteps she heard down the hall, for she was in no mood to deal with anyone. She lifted her eyes up from the hardwood floor. Her heart began racing as she noticed a person standing in the doorway. It took Chantal a few seconds to realize it was merely her own boyfriend.

"Andy, what is wrong with you?" she asked and rose from the sofa. "You look drunk."

"Whatever, Chantal," Andy snapped and put his head down.

"You know, ever since you got knocked out you have been a completely different person," Chantal said accusingly.

"Hey, I don't know why you're pissed at me when you're the one who spent the night with your ex," Andy snapped.

"Don't even go there," Chantal said and crossed her arms. She stepped closer to Andy. "I spent the night talking to an old friend whose girlfriend might have been kidnapped. We didn't even sleep in the same room. Don't throw out wild accusations."

"You know as well as everyone else that Jon doesn't care at all about Katherine," Andy spat.

"Well, at least Jon cared enough to listen to me cry about *you*," Chantal stated coldly.

"Why were you crying over me?" Andy questioned her.

When he looked up at her, Chantal noticed how red his eyes were. *You're stoned out of your mind right now,* she realized. *Really? Again? Why do you always revert back to that crap?* She looked at him with disgust. "Andy we've been together for, what, fifteen months? In that time, I have never felt this distant from you. I feel like you don't even want me around."

Andy stared at her blankly.

"Do you have nothing to say?" Chantal asked as a stream of tears plunged from her left eye. "Am I right?"

"Oh, no, Tal! Not at all!" Andy exclaimed, seeming to escape from a daze. "I love you as much as I always have."

"Then what is your problem?" Chantal asked. "Why are you sending me mixed messages?"

"Chantal, if I am, it's completely unintentional, and I'm sorry," Andy apologized and took a few steps closer to her. "It's so hard for me to see you with Anderson. I trust you completely, but I just get jealous. I suppose it's based on my fear of losing you."

"That's pretty much how I feel when Leslie hangs all over you," Chantal said and turned away from Andy.

"Well, you and Jon have history," Andy said and turned Chantal around to face him.

"So, maybe I think you and Leslie could have a future," she said and pushed past him.

Chantal nearly collided with Leslie when she turned to leave the sitting room. She had no idea how long Leslie had been in the doorway, but the smug expression on her face gave Chantal the impression that Leslie had overheard their argument.

Tears streamed down Chantal's face as she leaned against the wrought-iron railing that wrapped around the second-floor balcony. The beautifully maintained mansion represented nothing other than sadness. It seemed like Leslie had been going out of her way to make Chantal feel uncomfortable. It broke Chantal's heart whenever Leslie draped herself all over Andy and he did nothing to push her away. Resting her chin in the palm of her hands, Chantal glanced blankly at the forest ahead. It was quite depressing to think that she was trapped on a deserted island with a girl who practically wanted her out of the picture.

A sudden movement in the woods caught Chantal's attention. Leaning over the balcony, Chantal peered through the evergreen forest. There was a person running rapidly from tree to tree. Realizing that it was Katherine, Chantal opened her mouth to yell to her friend. She was unable to complete a single word before she collapsed to the ground.

Running her fingers down the mahogany railing, Leslie strode down the grand staircase of the two-story foyer. Her smile expanded with every step. Her display the night before had been a success. It had not only intrigued Andy but also increased the tension between Chantal and him. *Everything seems to be falling into place—except for Katherine,* she thought. *Well, with everyone out searching for her, Andy and I could at least have some alone time.*

"Hey, Anderson? Have you seen Chantal?" Andy asked as he stumbled into Jon on the main stairs.

"Hey, watch your step, dude," Jon warned him as he backed away from Andy.

"Sorry, I just figured she fled to you or something. She tends to do that when she's upset," Andy replied caustically.

"The last time I saw her, she was upset because you're an idiot. I can't find her anywhere now," Jon said and walked up a few steps past Andy.

"Oh, so you've been looking for my girlfriend?" Andy questioned him accusingly.

"What did I just say?" Jon retorted, without turning around. He turned left at the landing in the staircase and blocked out Andy's response.

Even though it had always bothered Jon to see Chantal with Andy, he had been able to be happy for her. Andy had always been a good kid, filled with morals and all of the other qualities Chantal deserved in a boyfriend. Lately, Andy seemed only capable of upsetting her with his newly self-centered approach to life. Nothing irritated Jon more than seeing Chantal distressed.

Jon began searching the East Wing from head to toe. He was determined to find Chantal. All five of the East Wing's bedrooms, the two bathrooms, and the sitting room were vacant. Jon knew that Chantal was curious, but he highly doubted that she would have gone off to explore the mansion alone. With a psycho on the loose, Jon barely felt secure enough to venture through the mansion alone.

Off of the East Wing, there was a narrow staircase that led to the third floor and attic. Even in daylight, the stairway seemed eerily dim. Hesitantly, Jon crept up the stairs and began brushing the walls for a light switch. Jon's left hand met with a switch as he neared the top step. After flicking the switch, Jon remained engulfed in complete darkness. He sighed; Chantal would never be in darkness.

Turning back down the staircase, an eerie sensation spread through Jon's veins. Shivering, Jon sensed a presence lurking behind him. As his heart hammered against his chest, Jon whipped around to face whomever was behind him. Surprisingly, Jon's eyes met with no one. Cautiously continuing down the stairs, Jon tried to convince himself that the paranoid feeling of being watched was only a result of his anxiety.

Descending toward the second floor, Jon noticed that each step made its own distinct creak. Pausing toward the bottom of the stairs, Jon felt the tiny hairs on the back of his neck rise. In his stillness, the creaking had continued.

Breathing heavily, Jon rushed down the remaining steps. As he stepped onto the bottom stair a loud crash erupted above his head. "What the—!" Jon exclaimed and leaped from the step. Without any hesitation, he darted down the hall.

"Jon, what's going on?" Lisa asked, appearing at the top of the main staircase.

"Upstairs… have you ever been up there?" Jon huffed in exasperation.

Lisa eyed Jon suspiciously. "What's going on upstairs?"

"Look, people are disappearing, and there are a lot of strange noises coming from the third floor," Jon cried and threw his arms out in front of him.

"So, let's check it out," Lisa said coolly and linked arms with Jon. Without giving off any sign of apprehension, she led him to the narrow stairs. "Is there a light or anything?"

"There's a switch at the top, but it doesn't work," Jon replied and followed Lisa into the darkness.

"So, what exactly did you hear?" Lisa asked.

"There was just some scuffling and thumping," Jon replied. "It all came from behind this wall," he added as he tapped on the wall to his left.

Schreeeeeeeeeech.

"Like that?" Lisa asked and halted abruptly in her tracks.

"Something like that," Jon replied as he shook a chill from his spine. He couldn't help but admire Lisa's fearlessness.

"What could that be?" Lisa asked and proceeded up the narrow stairway. After lightly pressing her foot onto the top step, Lisa slammed her body against the left wall. "Ewwwwweeee!" she exclaimed.

Jon's heart skipped a beat as he glanced down to the small pile of blood at Lisa's feet.

Lisa remained frozen, in utter silence.

"Lisa?" Jon questioned her as he studied her dazed expression. "Let's get out of here."

Escaping her daze, Lisa turned to Jon with protruding green eyes. "I can't believe this is happening… Go! Go! GO!"

Chapter 7

Chantal woke up suddenly, shivering and gasping for air. Realizing that she had no idea where she was, she instinctively jumped to her feet. "Ouch!" she exclaimed as she hit her head on the unexpectedly low ceiling. Engulfed in darkness, Chantal fell back to her feet and began to sob.

Andy sat on the bed Chantal had slept in and pulled his knees tightly to his chest. He stared out the nearby window, aimlessly wondering how his life had become so chaotic. So many things did not make sense.

Why would Leslie's parents allow us to stay alone at their cottage? Why did Katherine and Bobby break up? When did Katherine start associating with Jon Anderson? Why is there tension between Chantal and me? Why am I suddenly attracted to Leslie? Why would Leslie like me? Why did I get high with Lisa? Why do I keep losing my temper? Have I completely lost all of my social skills? I can't even talk to Chantal without making her cry. Why do I doubt my love for her? I love her! What is wrong with me?

Why can't I remember anything? Why do Lisa and Leslie seem more concerned with their fight than Katherine's safety? What in the world was Lisa trying to tell me? Why did my parents let me go away with my girlfriend? How did Chantal get permission to come away with me? Why would I even consider cheating on her? Why do I feel like such a scumbag? I would never cheat on Chantal, and I don't care that we don't have sex. Why do I suddenly feel like I should be having sex? I'm only fifteen—what is wrong with me?

Why don't I feel like myself? I would not normally think these things. I would never act this way! What happened to my morals and my desire to be a good boyfriend? I feel so distant from Chantal. What is this crazy world I have woken up in? I just want to think like myself again. I feel possessed—like I have no control over what I am doing. I know I shouldn't flirt with Leslie, and I know that I shouldn't be mean to Jon. I should actually thank him for doing my job. At least someone is taking care of my girlfriend. Why are my thoughts so disoriented? Maybe I need some sleep. When do I get to leave this place? Why don't I remember leaving Montgomery?

Andy closed his eyes and took a deep breath.

Bobby, Lisa, Leslie, and Jon sat nervously conversing in the second-floor sitting room. A half hour had gone by since Jon and Lisa had seen the blood on the stairs. They had split up and searched through the mansion, but Chantal remained missing. They had concluded that unless she was hiding between the wall studs, she was no longer under the same roof as them.

"Just let Andy sleep," Bobby said. "He's probably all banged up from the hit he took last night."

"Yeah, but we need all the help we can get to find Kat and Chantal," Lisa argued. "You didn't see the blood! I stepped in it. It's real."

"That blood could have been from an animal," Leslie said and glared at Lisa. "There is no need to jump to the conclusion that we are in danger."

"Leslie!" Lisa cried and shot her a piercing look. "I think enough is enough. This adventure should be ending right about now."

Leslie eyed Lisa with confusion and then turned to face the boys. "I want to leave here just as much as anyone. That's why we need to find Katherine and get back to my cottage. My parents are going to be there in two hours."

"How do we know Katherine isn't at your cottage?" Jon asked. "She's been there before, so I'm sure she knows her way around. What if we really aren't on an island? Why did we believe that guy, anyway?"

"It looked like an island to me," Bobby said. "I spent the entire night searching the woods for Katherine. Every path I took led to the water."

"Why would someone build a house on a deserted island?" Jon wondered aloud. "Why was it left unlocked? Nothing that is happening is making sense. If we didn't have to find Katherine and Chantal, I would be running back to Montgomery right now."

"I think you're right, Jon. I don't think we're on an island at all," Lisa stated firmly. "I think that guy was just trying to scare us. Katherine probably found her way back to Leslie's cottage, and we should concentrate on finding Chantal."

"Are you kidding me, Lis?" Bobby shouted angrily. "I searched everywhere for a way to the mainland. We are surrounded by water."

Lisa rolled her eyes. "You also searched everywhere for Katherine and couldn't find her. She's vacationed here with Leslie *numerous* times. She knows where she is going. Leslie, why don't we call your cottage to see if she's there?"

Leslie rose from the couch and walked over to the antique telephone on the cherry end table. "There's no dial tone," she said as she brought the phone to her ear.

"Interesting," Lisa said dryly.

"Well, I guess that makes sense, if no one lives here," Bobby reasoned aloud.

"*If* no one lives here," Lisa stated.

"What do you mean by that?" Bobby asked eyeing Lisa uncertainly. "You seem skeptical of everything we believe."

Lisa shook her head. "You have no basis to believe what you believe. Accepting things at face value is not always the wisest way to live."

"Lisa, if you have something to say, why don't you just come out and say it?" Leslie challenged her in an irritated voice. "You're implying a bunch of things, and I highly doubt there's any substance behind them."

Lisa stared at Leslie in dismay and dropped her jaw slightly. "Do you really want me to tell you what I think? Like, what I truly think is happening?"

"Yes, I do!" Leslie exclaimed.

"I think everything that has happened to us has been planned," Lisa said flatly. "Katherine is probably on her way here right now, after spending the night at your cottage. Her disappearance certainly brought a lot of people's true feelings out."

"That's a harsh accusation, Lisa," Bobby commented.

"Wait. Let me get this straight," Jon said and shook his head. "You think Katherine disappeared on purpose, so people would see who cares the most about her?"

Lisa shook her head. "No. I don't think Katherine planned any of this. What was meant as an adventure has turned into a game of deception—a game that I am sick of playing!"

"There you go again, implying things left and right and making no sense at all!" Leslie yelled and stomped her foot on the hardwood floor.

"The fact is, no one would leave this house unlocked—okay! Obviously, something strange is going on. I know for a fact that we are not on an island. If I didn't feel that it was urgent to find Chantal, I would lead you all back to Leslie's cottage right now. I've been here before, and Leslie has, too. Stop being naïve!" Lisa exclaimed and stormed out of the sitting room.

"You've been here before?" Bobby asked and turned to face Leslie.

"Yeah, it's my neighbors' house," Leslie replied coolly. "My family has been coming up here since I was three. I never said that I hadn't been here."

"Then, why do you think we are on an island?" Bobby questioned her.

"Well, any time I've come here, I've always gone over the bridge," Leslie replied. "If Lisa and Katherine know another way out of here, then they have one up on me."

"Okay, so there is hope that Katherine is safe," Bobby said. "That makes me feel a lot better. I just wish we had a way to get in touch with her."

"Well, what if I stay here in case Katherine or Chantal shows up?" Leslie offered. "You two can ask Lisa to show you the way to my cottage. You can look for both of them on the way and then see if Katherine is at my place. If my parents show up, stall them and say we're out for a walk or something. They *cannot* know that we spent the night at my neighbors' house!"

"Sounds like a plan to me," Jon agreed. "I just don't want to sit around doing nothing. I'm worried about Chantal. There is no way she's back at the cottage. She doesn't know her way around here at all, and the only person she would have gone off with is passed out in the other room."

CHAPTER 8

Andy rolled onto his back and creased open his eyes. He stretched his muscular arms over his head and yawned loudly. "I thought you were going to sleep all day," a voice suddenly spoke.

Wide-eyed, Andy darted his head to the right. Lying next to him in bed was Leslie, staring at him with her fierce green eyes.

Andy sat up immediately. "What are you doing?!" he exclaimed. "Why are you in here?"

"I was going to take a nap with you," Leslie replied and smiled sweetly. "We are the only ones here. Everyone else went out to look for Katherine."

"Why didn't you guys wake me up? I wanted to help look for her," Andy said, feeling disappointed.

"Bobby said to let you sleep. He thought you were beat up from last night," Leslie replied and inched closer to him.

"Even Chantal went without me?" Andy questioned her, lowering his eyebrows in confusion as he tore his eyes off of Leslie.

"She's not here," Leslie sang. "It's only me and you."

Andy stared blankly out the window in front of him. *Don't do it. Don't do it,* he heard a voice inside of him say. *Chantal loves you. Adam is your friend. You love Chantal. Don't even look at Leslie!* Suddenly an even stronger voice, one he had never heard before, spoke from inside of him. *This is the prize that you deserve. Don't let your good duties go unrewarded. Chantal likes Jon; saving yourself for her is pointless. She will never be able to please you; her heart is elsewhere.*

Andy grabbed hold of his head and began breathing deeply. "What is wrong with me!" he suddenly cried out.

Leslie jumped and appeared startled by Andy's outburst. "Andy, you know the truth," she said a few seconds later. "I know you can see what everyone else can see. Chantal likes Jon, so saving yourself for her is pointless. She will never be able to please you, Andy. Her heart is elsewhere."

Andy dropped his hands from his head and turned to face Leslie. "What did you just say?" he trembled as he felt the color drain from his face.

"I'm the prize that you deserve," Leslie sang softly. "You've done so many good things for everyone. Why do you always put yourself last?"

Andy swallowed hard as sweat began pouring from his forehead. "Why are you saying these things to me?" he questioned her nervously as tears began to fill up his eyes.

"Is what I say not true?" Leslie asked as she gazed at him with dancing eyes.

With superhuman strength, Andy hurled himself toward Leslie. It happened so fast that he felt like he was watching himself in a movie. As he watched, he knew what he was doing was wrong. He knew that he did not want to be doing it. He had no power to stop himself and no control over what was happening. Every ounce of him was screaming, "Stop!" Andy watched in horror, realizing that he was powerless over his own actions.

CHAPTER 9

With ease, Lisa led Bobby and Jon through the thick woods and fallen leaves behind the mansion. She was grateful that Jon and Bobby had been able to leave their differences behind them—at least temporarily. It was clear that everyone wanted to find Katherine, and out of respect for her, no one should be fighting.

There was little doubt in Lisa's mind that Katherine was safe. Lisa's main concern was Chantal. Lisa knew that Leslie wanted Chantal out of the picture, but she had never expected Leslie to actually take Chantal out of the picture! If Leslie had nothing to do with Chantal's disappearance, then they all had much bigger problems than a deceitful and envious "friend."

Lisa and Katherine had vacationed many times at the Lucus family's cottage. Leslie's family was quite large, and because the cottage could only comfortably sleep eight, the girls had often stayed at Leslie's grandparents' house. The best thing about Leslie's grandparents' house was that it had a bunch of trails in its surrounding woods. One summer, the girls had found what they thought was a cave. They had snuck out to explore it each night after dinner. The cave had turned out to be an old series of wells, but the thrill of exploring it had never left the girls. Since they had always walked to Leslie's grandparents' home from Leslie's cottage, Lisa recalled how surprised she had been when she and Katherine had discovered the main road that led to the estate.

Leslie's grandparents had designed their house with maximum privacy and security. Off of the main road, there was a small driveway that led to the gate of the estate. Through the gate, the driveway went underground and led to a private parking facility below the home. Lisa and Katherine used to joke that Leslie's grandfather must be in the mafia.

The truth was that Lisa, Leslie, and Katherine had always enjoyed exploring Leslie's grandparents' house. It was filled with secret passages, history, and luxurious possessions. Despite having over fifteen thousand square feet of living space, the mansion only suited Leslie's grandparents as a summer home. Nine months out of the year, the house stood vacant—well, normally.

It had taken Chantal an hour to calm down and decide that she was still inside the mansion. The steep slope of the ceiling led her to believe that she was somewhere in the attic. Wondering how she had gotten there scared her more than wondering how she would get out. She had exhaustively searched the walls surrounding her for any sign of a door, latch, or light switch. The only button she found did nothing when pressed. Intriguingly, the wall in front of her had an indentation, like a boarded-up window. No matter how hard she pushed against it, it would not open. To her right, there was a rope that led to an overhead pulley. Tugging on it did nothing. Chantal sighed and slumped against the back wall.

"Oh my gosh!" Katherine exclaimed as she ran rapidly toward Lisa, Jon, and Bobby. "I found you guys!"

"Kat!" Lisa cried out excitedly as she rushed toward her best friend. She embraced Katherine tightly as tears began stinging her eyes. She heard Bobby, who was behind her, let out a loud sigh of relief.

"Thank God you are okay!" he shouted loudly.

"Me? I was worried about you guys!" Katherine said as she pulled away from Lisa and threw her arms around Bobby. Lisa smiled, happy to see Katherine in Bobby's arms once again.

"I spent the night by myself at Leslie's cottage," Katherine stated as she freed herself from Bobby's embrace. "I figured that you guys would come back there."

Jon slowly approached Lisa, Katherine, and Bobby, appearing almost hesitant. "How did you get back to Leslie's cottage?" he asked.

"I took this path to the street," she replied and walked over to Jon. "Leslie's cottage is only two houses away from here. I thought Leslie and Lisa would have led you guys back there once everyone found each other. When none of you came back, I got worried. I thought maybe that guy had called the cops or something."

"Wait," Bobby said, sounding as confused as Lisa had expected him to be. "This is not an island? There is a road and other houses?"

Katherine nodded and then looked at Lisa with a perplexed expression.

"Wow, Lis and Jon, you guys were right," Bobby stated and placed his arms across his chest. "I wonder why Leslie thought we were on an island."

Katherine laughed. "Leslie knows this isn't an island!" she exclaimed. "Her grandparents' summer house is right through those woods!"

"What?!" Jon and Bobby shouted in unison.

Well, I'm about to get ripped into, Lisa thought and let out a loud sigh.

"We spent the night at her *grandparents'* house?" Jon questioned Katherine in disbelief. "And you were safe the entire time? This makes no sense. Why would Leslie put us through that?"

"I spent the night in the woods, searching for you, thinking we were stuck on an island," Bobby said to Katherine. "Now, you're saying that Lisa and Leslie knew we were not on an island and let us be deceived by that crazy guy?"

Katherine darted her eyes at Lisa, looking as if Bobby's question had blindsided her. "I'm not saying my friends deceived you," she said slowly. "I'm just saying that I know my way back to the cottage from here. I didn't even think of you guys spending the night at her grandparents' house. I figured it would be locked."

Bobby shot a glaring look at Lisa.

"I tried to tell you guys that it wasn't an island," Lisa said. "I didn't want any part of this."

"Well, yeah. You *did* say that," Jon said. "Kat, the door was unlocked. Why would a nice house like that be unlocked?"

"Ten to one, Leslie ran and unlocked the door while you guys were all running from that psycho," Lisa proposed.

"I never thought of that," Jon said. "Wow, I feel really betrayed."

Bobby laughed disgustedly. "At least you didn't spend the night freezing in the woods," he stated with evident frustration in his tone. "That girl has a *lot* of explaining to do."

"What I don't understand is why that guy yelled at us. If this is Leslie's family's property, why did he freak out like that?" Katherine asked and glanced strangely at Lisa.

"Maybe he is the caretaker or something," Lisa suggested. "Maybe he didn't recognize Leslie."

"Lisa, why didn't you tell us that we were in Leslie's grandparents' house?" Jon asked, sounding more curious than accusatory.

Lisa sighed and then rolled her eyes. *Don't hate me,* she thought. "Leslie told me not to. She wanted it to be an adventure. She said that if you didn't know whose house it was then you would have a better time exploring it. You know her! She loves drama. I agreed, reluctantly—not expecting people to start disappearing."

"People? Wait. Who else disappeared?" Katherine asked. "Where are Andy, Chantal, and Leslie?"

Lisa bit her bottom lip and glanced to the ground. "I don't even want to begin to imagine."

"Are they *all* missing?" Katherine gasped.

"Andy is taking a nap back at the house. Leslie said she was going to stay downstairs in case you came to the house. We can't find Chantal anywhere," Bobby explained. "She and Andy had some sort of a fight, this morning. No one has seen her since."

"That's awful," Katherine said. "Lisa, you have no idea where she is? This wasn't part of Leslie's plan?"

Lisa looked up at Katherine and shook her head. "When we couldn't find Chantal, that's when I started to worry."

"That house is huge. Do you think that she found one of the secret passages?" Katherine asked. "Like the tunnel below the servants' quarters or the stairs up to the library?"

"We didn't look in any of those places," Lisa replied. "We weren't supposed to be familiar with the house."

"That is ridiculous, Lisa. I can't believe you agreed to be a part of something so stupid," Bobby stated angrily.

Lisa knew he was right; she deserved to be reamed out. Chantal was missing.

"Once we couldn't find Katherine, you two should have confessed the truth. Then, maybe, I would have slept last night and Chantal wouldn't be missing!" Bobby cried out.

"I'm sorry!" Lisa exclaimed, hoping that she sounded more earnest than defensive. "All I did was agree not to tell you guys who owned the house. I didn't plan out any adventure or lie to anyone."

"Let's just go back to the house and start searching through the secret passages," Jon proposed and turned back toward the house. "Secret passages? Am I hearing myself right? What the heck is this place?"

"I can't wait to ream Leslie out for this," Bobby stated crossly as he followed Jon's lead back to the house. "I bet she knew Katherine was at her cottage. That's why she wasn't acting concerned."

"You're right. She didn't seem worried at all," Jon agreed. "She doesn't seem worried about Chantal either. Maybe she knows where she is, too."

"Good luck getting that out of her," Lisa said. "The biggest mistake we made was leaving her alone with Andy."

Jon, Bobby, and Katherine paused simultaneously. In unison, they turned to face Lisa. Katherine looked perplexed; Bobby looked worried; Jon looked enlightened.

Chapter 10

Ten minutes later, Lisa, Katherine, Jon, and Bobby reached Leslie's grandparents' mansion. Upon entering the house, they decided to search for Chantal first and interrogate Leslie after.

"Okay, Katherine and I know where all the secret passages are in this place, so we'll split up. Bobby, why don't you go with Katherine, and Jon, you can stay with me," Lisa suggested.

"Um, why don't I go with Katherine," Jon said flatly.

"Sorry! I'm frazzled right now," Lisa stated quickly as she remembered that *Jon* was Katherine's new boyfriend. "Whatever! Let's just start searching."

"Jon and I can look upstairs. You and Bobby can stay down here," Katherine called out loudly as she led Jon across the foyer.

"Jon, remember the blood! Katherine, make sure you search the attic carefully!" Lisa hollered loud enough so that anyone upstairs would hear her. Lisa knew that most of the bedrooms had secret passages and that Katherine was ready to attack them all. In case Andy and Leslie were together, Lisa wanted to make sure they realized they were not alone in the house.

"So, where do we start?" Bobby asked Lisa as he glanced around the kitchen. "I had no idea that this place has secret passages. How many does it have?"

Lisa shrugged. "Six or seven that I know of. Some connect to each other, some go underground, and some are hidden rooms."

Bobby laughed. "This sounds like we're in a horror movie or something. Seriously, I didn't think houses actually had secret passageways. I left that idea with the Hardy Boys and Alfred Hitchcock."

"Come on! Let's go," Lisa said as she rolled her eyes and dragged Bobby into the foyer. *I'm going to ignore that horror reference, for now.*

Katherine led Jon into the bedroom that he had slept in the night before. "I used to stay in this room a lot," Katherine said as she walked over to the closet. "This closet has a staircase in it that goes up to the third floor. You would never know it, but there is an entire hidden room up there, filled with all sorts of junk!"

"I envy you somewhat," Jon admitted. "I wish my childhood was filled with secret passages and hidden rooms."

"This kind of stuff only happens in dreams and movies," Katherine said as a dazed expression coated her face. "Don't be fooled."

Jon watched with intrigue as Katherine opened the bi-fold closet doors and stepped inside. She walked to the back of the closet and stepped to her right. "Come on," she called as she disappeared behind a structural column.

To Jon's amazement, Katherine had disappeared through a doorway located strategically behind the column. He never would have noticed the doorway if she hadn't vanished. Jon followed closely behind Katherine up the narrow set of stairs. "Is there a light in here?" Jon asked, wondering what Leslie's grandparents had against illumination.

"Oh, come on! Exploring is way more fun in the dark!" Katherine cried out playfully and tugged on Jon's arm.

Jon sighed. "I could trip over Chantal and not even know," he complained. "There better be a light at the top."

"Are you happy now?" Katherine asked once she flicked a light switch at the top of the stairs.

"A bunch of junk is right!" Jon exclaimed as he walked into the storage room. "Then again, I'm sure my grandparents' attic looks the same."

"Well, I don't see Chantal, unless she climbed into one of these trunks," Katherine said and pointed to the large storage trunks piled in the far corner of the room.

"It's not like her to wander off," Jon said as he turned toward Katherine. "She was really upset about Andy. I hope she didn't leave the house."

"I didn't see her when I was wandering through the woods," Katherine said. "I don't think she would—"

BOOM!

"What was that?" Jon asked. His heart began hammering loudly against his chest as he watched the color drain completely from Katherine's face. That was the last thing Jon saw before everything went dark.

"This house is awesome!" Bobby exclaimed as he followed Lisa through a narrow passageway beneath the servants' quarters. "I wouldn't even know what to do with a house like this. Leslie's grandfather must be in the mafia or something."

"Ha, that's what I always say," Lisa said as she turned the corner. Wiping cobwebs off of her shirt, she added, "I haven't been down here in years."

"No offense, but I don't think Chantal would hang out down here. Maybe you thought this was a happening place when you were a kid, but I don't think Chantal would," Bobby commented.

"Awww, is Bobby scared?" Lisa teased him while glancing from side to side as she continued moving through the passage.

"I can't honestly say that I'd chill down here," Bobby admitted.

"We'll be back upstairs in a minute," Lisa promised as she led him toward a narrow staircase. "You will get to see my favorite part of the mansion: the servants' quarters!" Lisa led Bobby up the narrow concrete staircase with the guide of her flashlight. At the top of the stairs, they found a long hallway that was lined with built-in bookcases. The bookcases were packed tightly with books that looked like they had not been read in a hundred years.

"What are all these books?" Bobby asked as he meandered ahead of Lisa down the hallway.

Lisa shrugged. "I think they are part of Leslie's great grandparents' library. We never bothered to check them out. I guess books didn't interest us much as children."

Bobby laughed. "Do books even interest you now?" He pulled one of the books off the shelf. "Woah. This is weird. Were Leslie's ancestors freaks or something?"

Bobby's unexpected comment caused Lisa to halt in her tracks. She turned around and glanced at Bobby. "Why would you ask that?"

"Look at this book," Bobby said and handed her a heavy leather-bound book.

"Possessions and Demonic Forces," Lisa read aloud slowly. She squinted her eyes and dusted off the cover to make sure she was reading it correctly. Lowering her eyebrows in confusion, she whipped open the cover and began flipping through the yellowed pages.

"Are you sure you want to look through that?" Bobby asked and took a step back.

Lisa widened her eyes as she skimmed through the first few pages of the book. "Grab another one of these books off the shelf," she demanded and nodded toward the bookcase-lined wall.

Lisa watched as Bobby cautiously selected a book from the shelf. "I half expected the wall to spin around," he muttered as he glanced down at its cover.

"Ha, don't even joke. It probably could," Lisa said dryly and looked back down at the book in her hand.

"Well, I don't know which is worse, possessions or the history of this house," Bobby said timidly as he began flipping through the book.

"What do you mean?" Lisa asked and stepped closer to Bobby. As she leaned over his shoulder to catch a glimpse of the book, a vibe of fear shot through her body.

"Entertaining Incubus," Bobby read slowly. "Why do I think that has nothing to do with music?"

Lisa swallowed deeply. "I don't even want to read that!" she cried and forcefully closed the cover of the book in Bobby's hand. Immediately, she felt overwhelmed with anxiety.

"So, Leslie's great grandparents were freaks," Bobby commented as he placed the book back onto the shelf. "No need to bug out, Lis!"

Lisa stared at Bobby in horror.

"What is wrong with you?" Bobby questioned her as concern overtook his normally sarcastic tone of voice.

Lisa shook her head from side to side and dropped her eyes to the floor. "This house has a lot of history," she said quietly. "We shouldn't have come through here."

"According to the few pages I skimmed in that book, it sounds like this place was once a whore house," Bobby said. "Leslie's great grandparents must have been swingers."

"Bobby, your imagination is far too light to understand what that book was referring to," Lisa stated. "It's interesting that the person with the strongest faith is the one who disappeared."

Bobby laughed nervously. "Oh, you're talking about the demon book? I thought you meant the sex log I was just looking at."

"I'm talking about both books," Lisa stated flatly. "They go hand-in-hand. We should not be down here."

Bobby looked thoroughly perplexed, but Lisa offered no explanation—she couldn't.

CHAPTER 11

Jon grabbed Katherine's hand and pulled her through the darkness. He had experienced enough of the mansion to last a lifetime. Hoping that the lightbulb had merely blown out, Jon tried to calm his nerves as he cautiously descended down the narrow staircase. Katherine's hand trembled inside Jon's grip.

At the bottom of the staircase, Jon and Katherine stepped through the doorway and into the closet. The closet door, which they had left open, was shut. At the sight of the light shining beneath the closet door, Jon and Katherine let out simultaneous sighs of relief. Pushing through the closet door, Jon entered the illuminated bedroom. Bright sunlight shone into the room through the glass doors to his right.

Jon watched Katherine's eyes grow large as she looked toward the balcony. "I just remembered something!" she cried. "When I was running through the woods, I thought I saw someone on this balcony." She rushed toward the glass doors. "I only looked up because I had always stayed in this room. For a split second, I thought I saw a girl leaning over the railing. I blinked my eyes and then she was gone. I thought it was my imagination."

"Are you serious?" Jon asked and followed Katherine through the glass doors and onto the balcony. "Do you think she fell over?" he gasped and hesitantly glanced to the ground below. A huge sigh of relief left his body when he observed the barren shrubs below.

"It really could have been my imagination," Katherine said. "Was Chantal wearing a green—"

"What are you two doing?" an accusatory voice sounded from behind them.

Jon's heart skipped a beat as he jumped to face the perpetrator.

"You scared the crap out of me," Katherine said to Leslie.

"What are you doing?" Leslie repeated as she stared intently at Katherine.

"That's it? That's all you got? No, 'oh Katherine you're safe! I'm so happy you found us!'" Jon cried.

Leslie shot Jon an icy look and then placed her eyes back on Katherine. "I'm happy you're okay," she said flatly. "I just didn't expect to see anyone standing on the balcony. I was startled. How long have you been up here?"

"Just a little while. We're looking for Chantal," Katherine replied defensively. "You didn't happen to shut the closet door in the bedroom a few minutes ago, did you?"

"Yeah, why?" Leslie asked curiously.

Jon sighed with relief.

A look of paranoia coated Leslie's face. "Why?" she repeated haughtily.

"We just heard a door slam; that's all," Jon replied quickly.

"Yeah, it startled us," Katherine chimed in.

Good response. From Katherine's words, Jon realized that she didn't want to share their experience with Leslie either.

"Oh, sorry," Leslie said and relaxed her facial expression. "I was in the other room, talking to Andy. He's sleeping again. I didn't realize I shut the door so loudly. I should go make sure I didn't wake him." Immediately, Leslie stepped off of the balcony and back into the bedroom.

"She's acting weird," Katherine said quietly. "Maybe she thinks I told you this is her grandparents' house."

"We need to find Chantal before we get into any of that," Jon said. He was utterly disgusted with Leslie.

"Leslie's grandparents are pretty nice people," Katherine said hesitantly, "but I never felt comfortable in this house. When we were little, we used to play in the old servants' quarters and hide in the secret passages. Lisa and Leslie thought it was exciting; I hated every second of it. At night, I used to crawl in bed with Lisa or Leslie. I always had terrible nightmares when I slept alone."

"Really?" Jon asked and leaned against the balcony's railing. He found her confession interesting. "Do you think this house is haunted or something?"

Katherine took a deep breath and raised her eyebrows. "All I can say is that I felt much safer alone in Leslie's cottage last night than I ever did under this roof."

⁂

Lisa and Bobby made their way into the living room of the servants' quarters and sat down on the cloth-covered sofa. Lisa put her head in her hands and began breathing heavily. Tears threatened to fill her eyes as she fought off the images flashing through her mind.

"Are you okay?" Bobby asked nervously. Lisa felt his hand upon her back. "Lisa, what's wrong?"

Lisa was unable to answer Bobby; she was in a different time and place altogether. Suddenly she was eleven years old, sound asleep in the mansion's bedroom of her choice. She was dreaming of her mother—even though she had barely known her. In her dream, her mother was beautiful, cheerful, and singing a lullaby of some sort. Lisa felt mesmerized by her, amazed by her beauty and charisma. She longed to reach out for her and feel her warm embrace. A lifetime without a mother's touch had left Lisa empty inside. She reached for her mother's hand and remembered how soft her skin had felt. Her mother turned to her and extended her arms around Lisa's petite body. Lisa remembered the warm feeling of her mother's embrace and how vivid it had felt. A warm vibe had shot through Lisa's body that she identified as the best feeling she had ever experienced.

When she awoke suddenly from her dream, she recalled being confused as to where she was and had trouble discerning reality from illusion. She could not understand why she still felt as though she was being held in someone's arms. She remembered trying to sit up in bed and feeling a presence lurking on top of her. Instantly, she felt suffocated and suppressed. No matter which way she struggled, she was unable to move. The embrace that had initially felt warm and comforting suddenly felt oppressive and forcefully restraining.

She had tried to scream but was unable to verbalize a single syllable. She had never felt so helpless in her life. She felt as though the breath of life was being sucked from her nostrils. Surely, the room was closing in on her. She remembered the faint light of the moon that

57

shone through the glass doors. She felt desperate for the light. Pinned down to her own bed, Lisa had been unable to wipe away the tears from her horror-stricken eyes. At eleven years old, Lisa had felt more violated than she ever did in her entire life. If Katherine had not suddenly burst into her bedroom, Lisa wondered if the oppression would have ever left her. She had never been happier to see Katherine in her life.

Lisa knew she could not allow the presence inside of the mansion to suppress her any longer. Truth be told, she had felt oppressed ever since she first stepped into the mansion—six years prior.

CHAPTER 12

Leslie sat quietly, mesmerized by Andy's beauty as she watched him sleep. Finally, the boy who had captured her every thought for the past few months had become her own. Leslie had never imagined the small argument she had overheard between Andy and Chantal would cause Chantal to leave the mansion. Although Leslie was somewhat curious as to where Chantal had gone, she was far too ecstatic over Andy's sudden interest in her to be concerned.

"So, what do you think it is about this place that gives people nightmares?" Jon asked as he followed Katherine down the second floor's West Wing.

Katherine shrugged. "I don't like to think about it. It gets my imagination going in a negative direction."

"Oh, sorry," Jon said quietly and put his head down.

"It's okay. I mean, I can answer you. I just get freaked out," Katherine admitted and took hold of Jon's hand as she stepped onto the third-floor staircase. "Leslie told me that her family learned how to overcome the nightmares. Years and years ago, they started keeping a diary and recording all of the weird things that happened here. Supposedly, the book is still lying around somewhere, but I've never seen it. Leslie's great grandparents moved into this house in 1910. Some of the diary entries date all the way back to then."

"Are you sure Leslie didn't make that up?" Jon asked.

"I don't think so," Katherine said and shook her head. "Her great grandparents were able to find peace in this house, and when they died, they left the house to Leslie's grandfather. Her grandfather decided not to live here year-round because he did not want to subject his children to the things that he had faced growing up. From what I understand, Leslie's grandmother found the diary and became horrified. She took it to a nearby church to get a pastor's opinion, and supposedly, he came to the house and prayed in every room."

"Did the prayer help?" Jon asked, amazed by what he was hearing.

"I guess *something* helped her grandparents, but it didn't seem to do any good for guests like Lisa and me," Katherine replied. "Leslie has experienced some freaky things, too. I'm surprised she brought you guys here."

"That's strange. I had a great night's sleep," Jon said. "Chantal said she slept well, too."

Katherine shrugged. "Maybe you and Chantal have the same protection Leslie's grandparents found."

"And what might that be?" Jon asked.

"I don't know, but when you find out, tell me," Katherine whispered, before ascending up to the third floor.

⁂

Chantal sat with her knees pulled tightly to her chest. She had already let out every scream for help her voice would permit. All of her cries had gone unanswered. Silently, she began praying for God's help. Over time, her voice became audible. After fifteen minutes, she found herself crying out psalms and prayers with great passion.

"The Lord is my light and my salvation; whom shall I fear? The Lord is the strength of my life, of whom shall I be afraid?" Chantal called out. "Dear Lord, I pray, protect me from whomever is trying to harm me. The blood of Your son Jesus Christ covers me, Father, and I know that nothing can happen to me that You have not allowed. Lord, please deliver me from this captivity. I am scared and weak. I know that when I am weak You are strong, and I pray, Lord, please fill me with Your peace that surpasses all understanding. Calm my heart and my spirit. Bind the enemy! Lord, I pray for the safety of my friends in this dark place. I know that You are with me. Thank you, Lord. In Jesus name, I pray, Amen."

⁂

A few moments later, Bobby followed Lisa through the main floor of the mansion. After mustering up all of her strength, Lisa had pushed aside her fear and set her mind on finding Chantal. Even though Lisa had grown up without religion, she had done enough research to accept that the ongoing battle inside the mansion was spiritual. Some people would call it "a haunting," others might call it "ghosts," but Lisa knew that the oppressors had never been in human form. It was naïve to think that Leslie's ancestors haunted the mansion. Ghosts do not rape people in their sleep; they do not put thoughts that are unable to be dismissed in people's minds; they do not possess people to act in ways they cannot rationalize.

Lisa recalled many nights when she had crept down to the hidden library and read through Leslie's great grandparents' books. They had found peace in the mansion when no one else could. When Lisa learned of their method, she had contemplated trying it out herself. Although she believed in the ultimate protection, and the protector, she never had the ability to go forth and accept either. Something inside of her would not allow the topic to be sought after. Knowing all that she knew, Lisa thought there was a chance that Chantal could be safe. Chantal had the protection and a personal relationship with the protector. No demons could harass her unless they had permission from God himself.

Chapter 13

Jon and Katherine continued to cautiously explore the attic. "I didn't expect there to be so many rooms up here," Jon said quietly. "They should make this place into a hotel. It's huge."

"Oh, yeah right! The guests will start disappearing, one by one," Katherine said facetiously. "Or they'll wake up at night, thinking something sat down on their bed, only to find themselves completely alone in their room. Convincing themselves that they were just dreaming, they will fall back to sleep, until they feel their bed start to sink in. Then, they'll begin to wonder if they are going crazy."

Jon paused and stared strangely at Katherine. "I'm taking it that happened to you?"

Katherine bit her bottom lip and nodded. "I was so afraid to tell my parents. I thought they would think we did drugs or something."

"Well, I think some people here do drugs, but definitely not you," Jon commented.

"Oh, you mean Lisa?" Katherine asked as she tapped on a wall to her left. "Hear that? It sounds hollow, doesn't it?"

"No, I don't just mean Lisa. I ran into Andy before he passed out, and he was baked out of his mind," Jon replied while tapping his knuckles on the wall. "Yeah, it does sound hollow."

"Andy doesn't do drugs," Katherine said matter-of-factly. "He was probably just upset about his fight with Chantal."

Jon rolled his eyes. "I know you guys think he is perfect, but I'm telling you to watch out for him. I think he puts up a pretty good front, but I can see right through it."

Katherine shrugged. "You could be right. I don't really talk to Andy much these days—not since Bobby and I broke up. It's weird because Bobby and Andy are best friends. So, who knows?"

"Do you think there's something behind this wall?" Jon asked, purposely changing the subject from Bobby.

"Behind this wall is an elevator shaft. It's one of those small ones that carry food and stuff. You know, a dumbwaiter?" Katherine explained. "It opens up to the room next door. Rumor has it that when Leslie's great grandmother got sick, she would sleep in the room next door so no one else would get sick. Leslie's grandfather always referred to it as 'the hospital.' He said his mother claimed that the room had healing powers. They used the dumbwaiter to send meals up to her. She didn't like to see anyone—not even her husband—when she was ill."

"That's kind of weird," Jon said and lowered his eyebrows. "How could a room heal someone? Were Leslie's great grandparents some crazy religion or something?"

Katherine shook her head from side to side. "No, not at all. They were Baptist, I think. They were all about God and Jesus. I think they even built a chapel in the house. Supposedly, it's behind one of the walls of the hidden library, but we never figured out how to get in there. That's probably good, though; I wouldn't want to disrespect God or Leslie's ancestors by breaking into a sacred place."

"This is becoming really interesting," Jon said slowly. "You said before that they had protection. Do you think it had anything to do with the chapel or their faith?"

Katherine shrugged. "Maybe? I never really thought about that."

"It's just weird that you said they were all about Jesus and they slept peacefully in this house. Chantal is definitely *all* about Jesus, and she slept fine. I am a Christian; my walk isn't where it should be, but I am a believer. I slept great last night. Maybe, just maybe, that is what we have in common with Leslie's ancestors," Jon said slowly, piecing a puzzle together in his mind as he spoke.

"I believe in God, and I still had nightmares," Katherine commented. "Why did I have nightmares?"

"Well, I don't know. Have you ever asked the Holy Spirit to fill you?" Jon asked, hoping he did not sound like a weirdo to his new girlfriend.

Katherine raised her eyebrows and stared strangely at Jon. "No, I can't say I ever did that," she said after a moment. "That's a little too out there for my beliefs."

"Well, then that could be what it is," Jon said. "We all have a void in us that can be filled with a spirit. When I accepted Christ as my Savior, the Holy Spirit filled me. Now, no other spirit can move into that resting place. Does that make sense at all?"

"Jon, you are really scaring me," Katherine said and looked down at her feet. "Don't talk about that stuff around me."

Jon glanced strangely at Katherine, surprised by her rejection. "Katherine, the Holy Spirit is God in spirit form. There is nothing scary about that. When you pray, don't you say 'In the name of the Father, the Son, and the Holy Spirit?' Why does it scare you to hear me talk about the name you pray in?"

"Stop!" Katherine snapped and glared at Jon.

"Woah. I'm sorry, Kat. Geez," Jon huffed and backed away from his girlfriend. "I've never heard you freak out like that before."

Katherine stared blankly at Jon and took a deep breath. "No, I'm sorry. I have no idea why I just got so upset. Just forget about it. Here, I'll show you 'the hospital.'"

Jon eyed Katherine warily. She was the most soft-spoken girl Jon knew. He was surprised to hear her voice rise, let alone hear her scream so demandingly. Dating someone who believed in God was important to Jon, especially after his failed relationship with Julianna. Katherine had been raised Catholic and still attended CCD on a weekly basis. He had never expected her to freak out on him for mentioning the Holy Spirit.

Jon knew that being naïve to the spiritual realm and spiritual warfare was very dangerous. It left people vulnerable. *Vulnerable to… oh, wow, no… there was no way that…* Jon's mind suddenly went into overdrive, piecing the puzzle of this vacation together. *The mansion, Leslie's attitude, Chantal's disappearance, Leslie's ancestors, the night terrors, Katherine's outburst, Andy's inconsistent behavior…* Jon's eyes grew wide. More than ever, he needed to find Chantal.

"This is the sick room," Katherine said. Her words interrupted Jon's pondering. "I don't know why this room was so special to—Jon what is wrong with you?" she asked.

Jon shook his head and snapped out of his daze. "Oh, nothing. I'm just worried about Chantal," he replied quickly.

"Well, I don't see her in here," Katherine said as she entered the small bedroom. The room's décor was antique Victorian. The walls were lined with mauve and green floral wallpaper, and the furniture was dark cherry. The skylight in the ceiling let an abundance of natural light into the room. Perhaps that was why the air in the room felt lighter than it had throughout the rest of the mansion.

"I like this room," Jon said as he walked around the canopy bed. "I can see why Leslie's great grandmother wanted to stay in here. It has a nice feel to it."

"You're crazy," Katherine retorted and crossed her arms. "I actually feel uncomfortable standing in here."

Jon bit his bottom lip and stared at Katherine. "Well, if Leslie's grandmother stayed in here a lot, and the dumbwaiter comes here, too, maybe there are some other secret passages close by. I think Chantal would like this room. We should spend some time searching around in here," he said. He glanced at the large cross that hung above the bed. On the wall opposite the cross was a gold-plated dove, symbolizing the Holy Spirit.

"I don't think so," Katherine said. "There are other places up here we could look. Why waste our time searching for an unknown secret passage when I know of two others that we haven't looked in?"

"I see your point, but call it intuition; I have a feeling about this room," Jon stated firmly. "I know Chantal *very* well, and I'm almost certain that she is close by. I can almost feel it."

Katherine sighed and rolled her light grey eyes. "Jon, I want to find her, too, but I'm all set with searching through this room. Leslie's great grandmother probably died in here. It's just eerie!"

"You see, I don't get that feeling at all," Jon said. "This is the only room that I actually feel relatively safe in. The rest of the mansion has felt dark and eerie. Don't you feel that way, too?"

"This whole place freaks me out," Katherine admitted. "I don't feel a bit of peace anywhere."

Jon realized it was pointless to argue with Katherine. The battle taking place was not his own, and he was getting nowhere with spiritual conversation. "Katherine, can you just give me a minute in here? I kind of need a moment by myself."

"Why?" Katherine asked.

"Because I want to pray, and I don't want you to feel uncomfortable," Jon replied honestly.

"You can pray in front of me. I pray, Jon. It's not like I'm anti-God or anything," Katherine stated and stepped closer to him. "It's just that the whole spiritual stuff freaks me out. I'd rather not think about it—especially when I'm in *this* house."

Jon glanced apprehensively at Katherine. "Okay, if you're fine with it," he said as he knelt down at the bed. "I'm going to pray out loud, just so you know."

"Oh," Katherine said, sounding surprised. "Well, that's fine, too," she added.

Well, here goes, Jon thought as he silently prayed to God for strength. "Dear Lord, I come before you, asking you to lead me to Chantal. Wherever she is, Father, I know you can guide me there. I pray for this house and for all of the unclean spirits here to move on. Fill this house with your Holy Spirit. In the name of Jesus I command all unclean spirits to be gone—"

"Okay, you have to stop!" Katherine suddenly cried out.

Jon darted his eyes up at Katherine.

"Oh my gosh! Just stop it, Jon! I need to get out of this room!" she exclaimed and ran toward the door. Jon swallowed deeply, as his heart pounded against his chest. "Shut up!" Katherine cried as tears began streaming down her face. "Stop! Just stop!" The sight of Katherine horrified Jon. She slid to the floor at his feet and continued to cry hysterically.

"Please God, I ask you to release Katherine from the bonds of any demonic forces. Father, in Jesus' name I pray, place your hand upon her and deliver her from the bonds of the enemy." Jon's heart was pounding so hard against his chest that he could feel his ribs vibrating. Sweat began pouring from his forehead as he stared at Katherine, feeling petrified of her. "Lord, I ask you place your hedge of protection around me. In Jesus' name, I pray, Amen."

Jon took a step back from Katherine, who had remained on the floor by the door with her head down. She was breathing heavily and trembling. Jon sat down on the bed, and rested his forehead in his hands. After a moment of wishing that he had never left Montgomery, he lifted his head to see Katherine, standing in front of him.

Andy awoke suddenly and shot his eyes around the bedroom. He breathed heavily and began shaking. "What a horrible dream," he said aloud. He grabbed his chest as he observed the empty room surrounding him. "Oh my gosh," he sighed, reflecting on the dream he had just awoken from. He felt guilty even thinking about it. Andy took a deep breath and put his head in his hands. "I would never cheat on her," he said to himself. "Oh, thank God that was just a dream," he added as he exhaled deeply. "That's what I get for doing drugs."

"Bobby, I am going to sound like a lunatic if I even try to explain to you what is going on," Lisa said as she led Bobby through Leslie's grandfather's office. "Honestly, you're better off not even knowing. You're just going to think that I've smoked way too much weed and that I'm full of it."

"Try me," Bobby said. "I'm pretty open-minded about most things."

Lisa sighed. "Well, how open-minded are you about demons?"

Bobby's face fell and the color disappeared from his normally rosy cheeks.

"See, I'm not saying a word," Lisa sang and ducked into the fireplace. "Come on, forget about what I just said and follow me. This isn't a real fireplace. You'll see."

CHAPTER 14

Leslie excitedly rushed into Andy's bedroom while saying, "Hey! How did you sleep?"

Andy sighed. "I had some pretty messed up dreams. I'll say that much," he replied and hopped out of bed. The sight of Leslie made him feel so uncomfortable that he had to fight off the urge to throw her out of the room. "I'm going downstairs to find Chantal," he called while breezing past her.

⁂

"Jon, I am SO sorry. Please don't think I'm a freak," Katherine pleaded as she plopped down on the bed beside him. "I have no idea what just happened to me. I couldn't control my emotions. I didn't mean any of those things I said. I'm so scared." Tears began flowing from her eyes, as she rested her head on his shoulder.

Jon let out a huge sigh of relief and put his arm around his girlfriend. "This house is definitely haunted," he said and kissed the top of her head. "You just have to fight off the forces until we find Chantal and leave."

"How?" Katherine asked as she looked up at him with a helpless expression. "Can't you see why I slept at the cottage last night? I get anxiety like this every time I'm in this mansion. This has happened to me since I was nine years old. I thought if I stayed by your side, I

68 "

would be okay. When you started talking about God, it triggered something. I think someone got pretty mad at you, but it wasn't me."

"I understand why you are freaked out right now. I am, too," Jon stated nervously. "Seriously, I am *really* freaked out. Like, I don't even want to think about what just happened because it's so messed up. You just need to remember that Jesus died on the cross for your sins and defeated death. You need to believe that the blood He shed on the cross paid the price for your sins. If you can handle confessing that, and truly mean it, no unclean spirit can ever have power over you."

❧

"This is crazy. I can't believe I just crawled through a fake fireplace," Bobby stated as he followed Lisa through a dimly lit tunnel. "What room are we behind?"

"Look, I really don't feel like answering any questions," Lisa said in an irritated tone. "I just want to find Chantal and get the hell out of here. This has been the most messed up weekend of my life. This house brings back way too many memories that I really can't handle right now. I hope you understand. I just can't play tour guide."

"Okay, okay," Bobby said. "No need to flip out about it. I'm just having a hard time believing this is even really happening. I swear, I'm going to wake up any minute at home in Montgomery. Then I will laugh and try to figure out what I ate before I went to sleep."

"I hope this is a dream, and preferably someone else's dream," Lisa said, as she turned toward a narrow staircase. "This will take us upstairs to one of the bedrooms. Hopefully, we can find some of our friends. I want to make sure Andy is okay. I don't trust Leslie around him—especially in this house."

"So, Leslie has the hots for him or something?" Bobby questioned Lisa, sounding unsurprised.

"Um, yeah, I think she would rape him if she had the chance," Lisa remarked dryly. "It annoys me to no end. Andy is like my brother, and I can't stand hearing her talk about him. I finally told Andy some of the things that Leslie says, and he actually seemed flattered, which made me really mad because he has an awesome girlfriend and shouldn't risk losing her."

"Yeah, Chantal is great," Bobby agreed. "Wow, I need to give Adam a heads up about Leslie. Andy is his friend. That sucks."

Lisa rolled her eyes. "Leslie's out of control."

"Lis, where does this door go?" Bobby asked, suddenly halting on the stairs and pointing to a panel that was slightly ajar.

Lisa peered at the panel. "Hmm, that's strange," she said and pressed on it. "I never knew that there was a door here. I have no idea where it goes or why it's ajar."

"Do you want to check it out?" Bobby asked.

Lisa raised her eyebrows and took a deep breath. "At this point, I'm beginning to doubt that we are going to get out of here alive. Yeah, whatever. Why not? Let's check it out," she rambled while pushing the panel all the way open and stepping into its opening.

"Is there a light in here?" Bobby asked.

"There should be," Lisa replied while feeling the wall to her left for a switch. "We should have grabbed flashlights from the kitchen."

"Should we go back and get one?" Bobby asked.

Lisa sighed. "If there isn't a light, then I doubt Chantal came through here. I don't know her that well, but she doesn't seem like a lover of darkness."

"Yeah, that would be her sister," Bobby said sarcastically as he followed Lisa back down the creaky steps.

"Where is everybody?" Andy said aloud as he walked through the large, abandoned kitchen. As he shot his green eyes from the stainless-steel appliances to the dark cherry butler's closet, the hairs on his arms stood up straight. He whipped his body around and gasped for breath, in search of the eyes he had felt upon him. The walls appeared to be closing in on him, and his heart was pounding so heavily that it felt like the floor was vibrating. Andy brought his hands to his head and cried out, "Wake me up from this nightmare!"

"What was that?" Lisa asked. Without hesitation, she ran past the doors of the family room and down the long, richly carpeted hallway.

"That sounded like Rosetti," Bobby called out from behind her.

"Andy?" Lisa shouted as she stood in the middle of the foyer and glanced up the monumental staircase. She had recognized Andy's voice—even though she had never heard him sound so distressed. "Andy!" she cried out. She walked past the staircase to the hallway that led to the first floor's East Wing.

"Rosetti! Where are you, man?" Bobby called out loudly from directly behind Lisa.

As Lisa and Bobby approached the wide doorway to the kitchen, a dark figure lunged at them. On instinct, Lisa shrieked and sank to the floor. Bobby grabbed ahold of her, catching her before she hit the ceramic tile. In the blink of an eye, the dark figure vanished, and they were left alone in the dim hallway with only fear and anxiety.

Moments later, Jon eased open the closet door in the Victorian bedroom in which he and Katherine had remained. Jon's eyes grew wide as he took in the sight before him. The presumed "closet" was not a closet at all. Before him was a room larger than the bedroom to which his back was turned. Books lined the wall to his right, and sunlight poured in through the dormers to his left. The ceiling peaked at a variety of different angles, and the walls were painted a soft sage green. An oriental rug lay in the center of the room, across the wide planked hardwood floor. The only piece of furniture in the room was an antique mahogany desk against the wall to his left.

"I've never been in here before," Katherine said softly as she walked past Jon into the room. She smiled. "And they thought great grandma Lucus was sick in bed all those years," she laughed.

"Looks like she had an office of her own," Jon said and walked over toward the built-in, aged-cherry bookcase.

"Her family must have known about this room," Katherine said as she pulled open one of the desk's drawers. "Maybe this was her private sitting room," she suggested as she pulled a black and white photograph from the drawer.

"Katherine, look at these books," Jon called while running his fingers across a dozen dust-covered books on the middle shelf. "They are all books about healing and deliverance." He turned to her and motioned her toward him.

Katherine placed the photograph on top of the desk and joined Jon by the bookcase. "Was she a doctor, or a nurse, or something?" she asked.

Jon shrugged. "Maybe, but I kind of doubt it. These books look like they're about spiritual healing." Jon widened his eyes. "That's why they called this 'the hospital!' I bet she had the gift of healing! Wow, this all makes sense. Leslie's great grandmother must have healed spiritually sick people."

Katherine let out a short laugh. "You mean people actually do that?"

Jon nodded. "You said that they were really into Jesus, right? I can tell just from these books that they were. And that chapel you told me about? I bet you can get to it from this room. This is getting really interesting."

Katherine raised her eyebrows at Jon. "If you say so."

Jon stared blankly at the books ahead, lost in deep thought. There was no doubt in his mind that the mansion was oppressed. Oppressed, haunted, or possessed—people could call it whatever they wanted. Either way, there was an evil presence lurking throughout its halls. If the house had once been used to deliver spiritually sick people from demonically inflicted illnesses, no wonder Satan had a stronghold on it. As long as Satan could keep people oppressed and away from the truth, there was no threat of losing souls to God's kingdom.

Jon reflected on his own faith, acknowledging that he and Chantal were not under Satan's power. *That's why he hasn't been able to hinder us. Satan roams throughout the earth, waiting to devour all the souls he can. Anyone whose faith is in Christ cannot be devoured, for they have power through Christ over Satan's demonic kingdom. Anyone who is without Christ is without protection and without the promise of eternal life.* Thankfully, Jon had put his faith in Christ at a young age.

Jon knew that people often desired to remain naïve to the spiritual realm, in an attempt to block out its existence. That was a very dangerous way to live. An unknown enemy can do a lot more damage than a known enemy, because the victim does not expect an attack. Being uninformed about spiritual warfare causes the same type of vulnerability. Attacks will come, and people will have no way of defending themselves because they know nothing about their enemy. They will not be equipped with the weapons necessary to fight back nor with protective armor. *Remaining naïve to spiritual warfare is like entering blindly with your limbs bound into the frontline of war,* Jon reasoned.

Chapter 15

ndy spotted Lisa and Bobby as he ran into the hallway off the kitchen. "Holy crap! I'm glad to see you guys!" he exclaimed. "I swear something messed up is going on in this house. I just had the most screwed up dream. Then I came down here and practically had an anxiety attack."

Lisa's eyes widened. Andy knew nothing of Chantal's disappearance, nothing of her own nightmares, and nothing about the mansion's history. Lisa held up her finger, as if to say, "give me a minute," and then took a deep breath. "Andy there are some things that you need to know," she said slowly, after a moment. "Let's go sit in the living room."

Bobby and Andy followed Lisa into the formal living room off of the foyer. Taking a seat on the white leather sofa, Lisa pulled Andy down beside her. Bobby sat across from them on the loveseat.

"Okay, don't freak out until I finish explaining everything," Lisa began while placing her hand on Andy's shoulder.

"Okay," Andy agreed and eyed Lisa warily.

"This isn't some random person's mansion," Lisa said. "This is Leslie's grandparents' house."

"What!" Andy exclaimed. "Are you kidding me? Is that what you two were fighting about earlier? Is that what you were trying to hint to me? That's why she had that thick set of keys!"

Bobby and Lisa glanced at each other. *Well, that solves the mystery of the unlocked door,* Lisa concluded.

"So, this was one big joke? Is Katherine even missing or was that all part of the big scheme?" Andy asked as he anxiously darted his eyes from Lisa to Bobby.

Lisa sighed. "I told you not to freak out *until* I finished. No, Katherine wasn't part of Leslie's scheme, but we did find her. She is here now with Jon… looking for… Chantal." Lisa bit her bottom lip and put her head down as she spoke those last words.

Andy's eyes grew wide. "What do you mean 'looking for Chantal?' What happened to Chantal?"

"Look, we don't know. We've been looking for her ever since you fell asleep," Bobby stated flatly. "I'm sorry, dude. I can't make any sense of what has happened since we left Montgomery."

"So, you mean that psycho-guy could have her somewhere?" Andy asked, looking horrified by the thought. "Why didn't anyone wake me up? What the \$@%# is wrong with you guys?"

"Look, dude, you weren't even asleep for that long. I suggested that we let you rest because you didn't look like you felt too good. Then we went to look for Katherine. The psycho-guy isn't a threat, and we aren't even on an island. Katherine spent the night at Leslie's cottage waiting for us to come back," Bobby explained. "Just don't freak out, OK?"

Andy took a deep breath and put his head in his hands.

"While you were resting, we split up in the house to look for Chantal. None of us wanted to confront Leslie until we found Chantal, so we left her alone with you. She doesn't even know that everyone knows this is her grandparents' house," Lisa said.

Andy shot his head up. "What do you mean you left Leslie alone with me?" he questioned her as his green eyes grew wide.

"She wasn't with you?" Lisa asked, feeling momentary relief.

Andy shook his head from side to side. "I was asleep the whole time. I don't think she was in the room with me. I woke up and came right down here. I saw her on my way down and told her I was going to find Chantal. I didn't know Chantal was actually missing when I said that though."

"Are you sure about that?" Lisa asked after observing the paranoid look on Andy's face.

Andy glanced from Lisa to Bobby and then began rubbing his forehead. "You know what? I honestly have no idea what is going on here, or how I even ended up here, or why everything is so screwed up. I just want to find my girlfriend and go back to Montgomery."

"I'm with you on that, guy," Bobby said.

"So, what? This house is so big that you guys haven't checked all the rooms yet or something?" Andy asked.

"Andy, we checked the rooms. She isn't in any of them," Lisa replied flatly. "We have much bigger problems than that. This place has a ton of secret passages—some that lead to underground rooms. This house is insane. Katherine and I know it well, so we've split up and begun looking through the secret passages."

Andy laughed. "Secret passages?" he questioned her. "Come on, Lis! You've got to be kidding me. That is ridiculous!"

"Dude, she's not joking," Bobby spoke up. "We've been hunting through tunnels and everything. We even found this crazy library with all these books about sex and stuff. I feel like I'm in a horror movie."

Andy darted his eyes from Lisa to Bobby. "What are you guys not telling me?"

Bobby cleared his throat uncomfortably.

Lisa swallowed deeply and glanced to the floor.

"All right. I'll forget that you said anything about a horror movie, and I'll forget that I just saw a ghost in the kitchen and that I've had terrible dreams since I stepped foot into this place. We can just go on our merry way, hunting for my missing girlfriend, and if you guys want to tell me why this place makes me think I'm going insane, feel free," Andy rambled as he stood up abruptly.

Chapter 16

Katherine let out a loud gasp from inside the healing room's closet. "Jon, there are stairs in here!" she exclaimed.

Jon rushed into the closet and found Katherine standing at the top of a narrow set of stairs. "Wow, I bet those go somewhere good," he remarked and placed his hand on Katherine's shoulder.

"I wouldn't have noticed them if I didn't push all of these clothes aside," Katherine explained while gesturing toward the many old-fashioned dresses that hung on either side of the staircase. "They ran across this rod and completely covered the stairs."

"Oh, then there's got to be something good down there," Jon said excitedly. "I know Chantal is around here. She *has* to be." Jon had a gut feeling that Chantal was safe and that he was close to finding her. His faith allowed him to believe that even in traumatic situations, God was in control.

"So, let's check it out," Katherine suggested and took hold of Jon's hand. "What do we have to lose, right?"

Jon sighed. He was glad to have his levelheaded, optimistic girlfriend back.

⁂

Andy, Lisa, and Bobby took flashlights from the Butler's closet and headed to the fake fireplace. In complete disbelief that any of this was really happening, Andy followed Lisa through the small door on the inside of the fireplace. Finding himself in a dark tunnel, Andy suddenly understood what Bobby meant by "horror movie." Although the tunnel walls were painted and the floor was thinly carpeted, Andy still felt like he was somewhere in the house he should not be.

"So, is this freaking you out yet?" Bobby called from behind Andy.

"Um, you could say that," Andy replied, grateful that he was not the last one in line. "I really doubt Chantal would hang out in here, though."

"That's what I said earlier. She'd never explore this place alone," Bobby said.

"Unless she accidentally stumbled into one of the passages," Lisa remarked as she turned toward a staircase. "That's what I think happened—if she is actually in one of these places. In this house, you could easily lean against a wall and end up in a different room."

"Why would anyone design a house like this?" Andy asked as he attempted to shake a chill from his spine. "I feel like we're in a maze."

"Maximum security and privacy, that's for sure," Lisa replied. "To get to this place from the main road, you have to go through a tunnel. It's bizarre."

"I think I'm all set with hanging out with Leslie after this," Andy commented dryly as he followed Lisa up a few steps.

"Um, yeah. I think I am, too," Lisa agreed. "Like I told you before, she planned most of this because she wanted to hook up with you. I was afraid you had hooked up with her while we were looking for Katherine."

Andy swallowed deeply. "I would never cheat on Chantal," he stated sternly.

"I hope not," Lisa said and paused on a step. "Sometimes, this house makes you do things you can't understand."

Andy let out a quick laugh. "I wish you didn't just say that, Lis," he said while following Lisa through an ajar wall panel. "And I'm going to pretend you didn't."

⚜

Following closely behind Jon, Katherine slowly stepped down the closet's staircase. For five years, she had been petrified inside the mansion and had no idea why. Even though Jon's explanation had sounded far-fetched and abstract, Katherine was unable to dismiss it. From her personal experiences in the mansion—the nightmares, the visions, the feeling of always being watched, and the anxiety—she knew Jon's theory could be accurate.

"We should have grabbed a flashlight," Jon whispered as he stepped off the bottom stair. "It's really dark down here."

"Isn't there a light?" Katherine asked. She took hold of Jon's arm as she stepped into the dark corridor. The musty smell of the air and the cobwebs that lingered above her head made it obvious that the passage had not been cleaned in decades. *Odd,* Katherine thought. *The caretakers have upkept all of the other secret passages.*

"There might not have been electricity the last time someone came down here," Jon remarked.

Katherine took a step back from Jon and began running her small hand over the wall opposite him. The hallway that they stood in was only four feet wide but still far grander than any of the other secret passages. Wooden panels, carved with intricate details, lined the walls. With the absence of light, Katherine struggled to distinguish the type of wood or the design carved into each panel. Running a single finger through a crevice on one of the panels, Katherine traced her finger in the form of a cross. Just as she began telling Jon about her discovery, a flash of light shot down the hallway.

"Ahhh!" Katherine and Jon shrieked in unison. Katherine knew that neither of them were responsible for the sudden illumination. Katherine clung to the sleeve of Jon's shirt and gasped to catch her breath.

"What was that?!" Jon cried out while panting. "Did you see that?"

Katherine nodded intently as fear stole her ability to speak.

"Did you touch any sort of switch? Or a lever? Or anything?" Jon asked in exasperation.

"N-n-n-n-n-no!" Katherine exclaimed, struggling to find her voice.

Jon took a firm hold of Katherine's hand. Tugging her down the hallway, he hustled toward the origin of the light. His footsteps grew heavier, and his strides grew wider and wider, as he continued down the hall. Katherine imagined sweat seeping from Jon's forehead and a fiery look in his eye; she knew that he was at his wits end. By the time they neared the end of the hallway, Jon's footsteps had erupted into thunderous stomps.

Jon's rampage came to an abrupt halt as he reached the end of the hallway. Three beams of blinding light shot forth, sending Jon and

Katherine tumbling to the floor in panic. Seconds later, heavy footsteps rushed in their direction. Katherine and Jon scrambled to their feet and began slowly backtracking down the hallway.

"Katherine?" a female voice cried out, sounding louder with each syllable. "Jon? Is that you?"

Katherine glanced up at Jon, letting out a heavy sigh of relief as she recognized Lisa's frantic voice.

"Thank God," Jon sighed and rested his head against the wall.

"We're over here, Lis," Katherine called as she stepped out of the dark corridor and into the illumination.

Within three seconds, Lisa, Bobby, and Andy had reached Katherine and Jon. "I have never been happier to see you guys," Andy stated and patted Katherine on the top of her head. "Seriously, we thought you guys were ghosts or something."

Katherine let out a short laugh. "Well, you scared us half to death with your flashlights, but I'm so happy you have them. We haven't found any electricity down here."

"How did you get in here?" Lisa asked. "You didn't go through the stairs behind the office, did you?"

"No, not at all," Katherine replied. "You won't believe what we found in the attic, Lis. You know that old hospital room we never really went in?"

"Yeah," Lisa nodded and spread her eyes wide with curiosity.

"Well, there is a whole other room off of it that we never knew about. It's filled with old books about healing. Then, when I was looking in the closet, I moved some clothes aside and found a hidden staircase beneath a bunch of dresses. It led us down to this hallway," Katherine explained. "I have no idea where we are. Where did you guys come from?"

"The stairs behind the office. One of the panels on the wall turned out to be a trap door. Bobby and I found it and then had to go back to the kitchen to get flashlights because there was no electricity. That's where we found Andy," Lisa said. "That's so crazy that we ended up in the same place at the same time. I never thought we'd run into you; then again, I guess we are on the second floor. Sorry to freak you out."

"I think it's good we are all together," Jon said and glanced from friend to friend. "Chantal is nearby. I can feel it. I really think that this passage leads to the chapel Katherine told me about."

"I thought that was just a myth," Lisa said and lowered her eyebrows toward Katherine. "You really think there is a chapel?"

"Without a doubt," Jon replied quickly. "You'll have to take a look at the room we found upstairs. I've formulated a theory about this house, based on what I've felt, seen, and heard."

Jon and Katherine explained what had happened to them during their hunt for Chantal. Katherine supported Jon as he explained his theory and reasoning. Lisa told Katherine and Jon about the dark figure outside the kitchen and the books in the hidden library. Piece by piece, they began to put the puzzle together. Each story told provided more confirmation for Jon's theory.

After taking a deep breath, Lisa confessed some of her personal experiences in the mansion: the dream of her mother that had haunted her for years and the feeling of being raped in her sleep. Then Andy spoke up and shocked everyone with his words.

"When I fell asleep earlier, I was baked out of my mind," Andy admitted. "I had a dream that I woke up with Leslie lying in bed with me. She told me that you all went out to look for Katherine and that she wanted to take a nap with me. I was really confused as to why you guys would go without me, but Leslie told me that you had left us in the mansion. Then I started having these terrible thoughts that I didn't want to think at all—horrible, condemning, arrogant thoughts. Things I would never normally think. It was as though someone else was thinking for me. I tried to block them out and fight them off, but I couldn't. Then Leslie, in my dream, said the exact same horrible things that the voice inside of me had said a moment earlier. It freaked me out to no end, and I remember wanting to run from her, but I couldn't. Then it was like this force came over me, like I was thrown out of my own body and onto the sidelines. As a spectator, I watched myself forcefully take advantage of Leslie. Like, I watched myself rape her, and there was nothing I could do to stop it. It was horrible. It was the worst dream I have ever had. Then I woke up suddenly, more confused than I can possibly express, with my heart pounding. I was so happy to wake up because I realized it had all been a nightmare. It was so terrible that I actually still feel guilty—like I did something horrible to Leslie and Chantal. I know I didn't, and that I never would, but it felt so real."

Katherine was convinced that her expression mirrored Jon, Lisa, and Bobby's, who were staring at Andy with protruding eyes. The color had drained from Lisa's normally tan skin and tears had filled up her green eyes.

"Maybe that's why she acted so weird when she saw us on the balcony," Katherine said slowly and looked at Jon.

"What are you thinking? That it really happened?" Jon asked and gazed uneasily at Katherine.

"It was a dream!" Andy shouted defensively.

"Leslie told us that she had been talking to you, but that you had fallen back to sleep," Katherine explained. "That doesn't make any sense, if you were asleep the whole time."

"She could have lied," Andy replied matter-of-factly. "She lied to us about this house, so why should any of us believe her?"

"That's true," Katherine and Jon said in unison.

"Whatever, guys. Let's just keep looking for Chantal," Lisa spoke up. She appeared more disturbed by the possibility of Leslie and Andy than she had while telling her own stories about the mansion. Of course, Katherine hoped that Andy had not taken advantage of Leslie, but she couldn't help but feel that Leslie had somehow taken advantage of him.

CHAPTER 17

Andy, Katherine, Lisa, Bobby, and Jon proceeded slowly through the passage, pressing on every wall panel and periodically calling Chantal's name. As the end of the hallway drew near, the friends began growing hopeless.

"I wish we never stepped foot inside this house," Andy said. "This hallway leads nowhere special."

"Why would someone build such a grand passage that only leads to a bookcase?" Lisa asked as she walked up to the built-in, dust-covered, cobweb-lined shelves full of thick, leather-bound books. "We must have missed something."

Bobby's harsh words suddenly began running through Jon's mind: *"Take the person who matters most out of your life and then realize that they've vanished, knowing that if maybe you had done one thing differently, they could be safely in your arms. Try that, Anderson."* Jon's eyes widened. He certainly knew how Bobby had felt the previous night while searching hopelessly through the woods for his first love. Not even twenty-four hours later, Jon was walking in his shoes.

Jon began to wonder if Bobby had any part in Chantal's disappearance. Was it his way of getting back at Jon? Could Bobby and Leslie have planned it together? They had been together in the woods when they ran into Chantal and him. Jon quickly dismissed those thoughts from his mind. How could he even think such terrible things?

Bobby would never put Chantal in harm's way. He would never put Andy—his own best friend—through this type of trauma. Unless… unless Andy was in on it, too?! After all, Chantal had feared that Andy liked Leslie. *Okay, now I know I'm going crazy*, Jon thought. He felt like he had been placed in the game Clue. *Was it Bobby in the library with the candlestick, or was it Leslie in the conservatory with the knife?* At that point, he couldn't trust anybody and certainly not his own thoughts.

"Oh my gosh! I forgot! There was a cross engraved in the woodwork down that hall that you guys found Jon and me in!" Katherine suddenly exclaimed, breaking through Jon's contemplation. "I was about to point it out when your flashlights startled us. I wonder if that was a clue? Maybe the chapel is around there?"

"Take my flashlight and go check it out," Andy said and handed Katherine his flashlight. "I want to stay here and inspect this bookcase. I think it could be masking something important. Bobby, stay with me. The rest of you guys go with Kat. Just yell if you find anything, and we will do the same."

"Okay!" Katherine cried and grabbed onto Jon's arm. "I'm so glad I remembered that!"

Jon and the girls had only made it halfway down the hallway before he heard Andy let out an ear-piercing scream.

⁂

Chantal woke up, struggling to catch her bearings. Something had startled her in her sleep, something loud and frightening. Previously, while praying, a warm feeling had suddenly come over her, stealing all of her fear away and relieving her anxieties. The feeling had been so overwhelming, warm, and comforting that it caused her to fall asleep.

In her sleep, an angel had appeared to her, surrounded by blinding light. She had never seen an angel before—not even in her dreams—and found him more beautiful than she had ever imagined. He told her not worry and that the battle taking place was not her own. He said she was protected from the torments of the wicked one.

"You are in a dark place, Chantal, but a bright light shines within you—so bright that it overcomes every ounce of darkness. The darkness cannot comprehend such light; it actually fears the light. There is another source of light in this place. He, with an army of angels, is fighting his way through the dark powers of principalities to this holy sanctuary. Do not be afraid. The Lord is using you, and you will be blessed greatly. Shortly after you awake, your friends will find

83

you. Do not be deceived by the darkness that dwells within many of them. Keep your eyes on the light. You shall edify each other. Together, you will break many bonds of the enemy. Pray without ceasing, obey the voice of the Lord, and put on the whole Armor of God. You are on the winning team, for it is already finished." His words were dearer to Chantal than anything she had ever heard.

Suddenly, the small room that she was in began to shake. The pulley above her head began turning, and the room began descending as if it were an elevator. Just as Chantal's stomach began to drop, the pulley came to a screeching halt. The panel on the wall in front of her flung open. Light streamed into Chantal's eyes as she struggled to catch her breath.

"Chantal!" Andy's voice cried out. He reached through the small door and pulled her into his arms.

Chantal let out a sigh of relief and climbed out of the dumbwaiter shaft with Andy's aid. She had never been happier to see her boyfriend. Everything they had fought about earlier seemed trivial.

Without taking a glance at her surroundings, Chantal threw her arms around Andy. As she leaned in to kiss his cheek, a queasy feeling settled in her stomach. *Do not be deceived by the darkness that dwells within many of them.* Why had the angel's words suddenly come to her mind? Andy was the light; he had to be! He attended church with her weekly. He volunteered for every charity that he knew of. He gave himself completely to everyone he loved.

Chantal pulled free from Andy's embrace and stepped back to take in her surroundings. She was standing inside a small chapel; there was an altar to her right and three rows of pews to her left. The candles shining from the altar dimly lit the room. A large cross hung high on the wall straight ahead of her. Suddenly, Chantal understood what the angel in her dream had meant by "this holy sanctuary." *I've been inside a chapel all along?! Then that means an angel really did visit me!* Chantal's heart pounded heavily against her chest as she glanced uneasily from Andy to Jon to Lisa to Bobby and to Katherine. *Only one source of light? How could it not be Andy? He seems so righteous.* From within she heard a voice say, *beware of the wicked one who disguises himself as an angel of light.* Chantal's eyes widened.

"You seem really freaked out," Andy said as he stepped closer to her. "None of us know what happened to you or how you got here. From the look on your face, I can tell that you have no idea either. But you're safe now, and that's all that matters."

Chantal lowered her eyebrows and took a step back from Andy.

"Aren't you going to say anything?" Andy questioned her. "Are you in shock? I thought you would be happy to see us." He turned away from Chantal toward the rest of the group. "Is she in shock? What do people in shock look like? Did something happen to her?!" he asked them, sounding dismayed.

Chantal bit her bottom lip and stepped away from Andy and onto the altar. She bowed her head and began praying for guidance. She retraced her day—outside on a balcony and then suddenly inside a chapel's dumbwaiter. How could any of that be? She widened her eyes and swallowed deeply. Psalm 27, her favorite psalm, was coming alive to her.

The LORD is my light and my salvation; Whom shall I fear? The LORD is the strength of my life; Of whom shall I be afraid? When the wicked came against me to eat up my flesh, my enemies and foes, they stumbled and fell. Though an army may encamp against me, my heart shall not fear; though war should rise against me, in this I will be confident. One thing I have desired of the LORD, that will I seek: that I may dwell in the house of the LORD All the days of my life, to behold the beauty of the LORD, and to inquire in His temple. ***For in the time of trouble He shall hide me in His pavilion; In the secret place of His tabernacle He shall hide me; He shall set me high upon a rock.*** *And now my head shall be lifted up above my enemies all around me; Therefore I will offer sacrifices of joy in His tabernacle; I will sing, yes, I will sing praises to the LORD.*

"You know, don't you?" Jon suddenly spoke. Chantal turned to see him walking across the room toward her. "I've been fighting through darkness, worse than I have ever seen before, to get to you."

As Chantal looked up at Jon, a feeling of peace surged through her body. *Of course, Jon is the light,* she thought. Jon had been a Christian even longer than Chantal. She knew that even though Jon had backslidden in eighth grade, he still had faith. *It is faith that makes you right with God,* she thought. *Not good deeds.* At that thought, she glanced from Jon to Andy.

CHAPTER 18

Andy watched Chantal step off of the altar and throw her arms around Jon. "Pray with me," she said, "for all of them. There is darkness here, and we are the only sources of light. God is present because you and I are gathered in his name. Ready, Jon? Get on your knees." Without delay, she dropped to her knees in Jon's arms.

What does she mean, the only sources of light? Andy wondered. *I go to church with her every week. Anderson hangs out with Jason Davids! How could he be a source of light? Is she out of her mind?*

"Dear Lord, I pray for your hedge of protection around Jon and me. Please give us the faith that we need to perform this task and please fill this room with your Holy Spirit," Chantal prayed. The tears that began seeping from her green eyes startled Andy.

"Dear Lord, please fill Chantal and me with your Holy Spirit and the faith that we need to take up our swords against the darkness," Jon prayed out loud. He squeezed Chantal's hand as he spoke.

Don't touch my girlfriend like that, Andy thought angrily. He fought off the urge to interrupt Jon's prayer by pulling Chantal away from him.

"In Jesus' name, I command any unclean spirits to be gone from this house," Chantal demanded.

"In Jesus' name, I command every demon to be gone from this house. I am covered by the blood of Jesus Christ. Chantal is covered by the blood if Jesus Christ. The blood of Jesus Christ covers this room," Jon shouted.

"What are you guys doing?!" Bobby called out, sounding distraught.

"Let them pray," Lisa said and took a seat in one of the pews. "We need this. This house needs this."

Andy glanced strangely from Lisa to Chantal. He felt helpless, confused, and condemned. Everything around him grew hazy, and he struggled to make out Chantal's facial features. His feet suddenly felt incredibly light. He lost the ability to see anyone or anything around him, but he could feel air breezing by him and hear Chantal's sweet voice. He was tumbling through space.

"Chantal! Why can't I see you?!" Andy cried out helplessly. A moment later the fuzziness faded. Chantal's face came into focus. "Now I see you," he said quietly. Then he drifted off into sleep.

❦

An hour later, Andy shot his eyes open. He found himself in a small room, with multiple sets of anxious eyes staring at him. Chantal, Lisa, Bobby, Katherine, Jon, Leslie, his parents, and his brother Robby surrounded him. "What are you doing here, Mom and Dad?" Andy asked, attempting to sit up in bed.

"Oh, my son! My son! My baby!" his mother cried while rushing to his side. She began kissing his hands and forehead rapidly, as if she had not seen him in years.

Andy stared at his mother, wondering what was wrong with her and why his family was at Leslie's grandparents' house.

"Thank God you are all right! You're going to be all right, Andy!" his mother exclaimed as tears flowed from her eyes.

"Gina, give him some space," his father stated as he placed his hands on her shoulders. "The doctor said that he would be confused."

Doctor? Andy took another glance around the room, realizing it looked far too institutional to be part of a Victorian mansion. He glanced down at his body and became horrified by the sight of the wires, tubes, and machines that surrounded him. He darted his eyes at Chantal; she was standing at the foot of his bed, smiling widely with tears streaming down her beautiful face.

"What happened to me, Chantal?" he asked softly.

"You got hurt really bad," Chantal replied and walked to the side of his bed. "Do you remember the bad thunderstorm when we were at my house?"

87

"Wait, what? No, I mean what happened when you came out of the dumbwaiter?" Andy questioned her in bewilderment.

Chantal lowered her eyebrows and squinted in confusion. "Um," she stammered uncomfortably. "What? I don't know what you're talking about."

"What?" Andy asked. "Lisa, Bobby, back me up. We were all just there… at Leslie's grandparents' house on Fallen Lake… for my recovery celebration. Remember?"

"Recovery celebration? Recovery from what?" Lisa asked. The perplexed look in her green eyes made Andy rethink his confidence.

"From… from… from… I don't know. I don't remember," Andy stammered.

"Excuse me. I need you to all leave the room for a few minutes," a young man wearing a pair of light blue scrubs said upon entering the room. "The examinations and observations are going to take a while. Maybe you'd like to have dinner in the cafeteria? Mrs. Rosetti, we will page you once Andy can be seen."

Mrs. Rosetti nodded and glanced at Andy lovingly. "We'll be back soon. You make me so happy, Andy. So happy."

Andy eyed his mother warily and then watched the rest of his family and friends exit the room. He stared at the doctor, hoping he would be able to answer the many questions running through his mind. Even though Andy had no idea where he was or why a doctor was examining him, he was relieved to be out of the mansion. Chantal's prayers must have helped him, somehow.

***

Andy's face lit up when Chantal, his parents, and his brother crossed the invisible threshold into his room just after seven o'clock. "Hi, guys," Andy said quietly. He found it difficult to propel his voice.

"Hey," Chantal greeted him. Her face radiated with joy as she made eye contact with him.

Andy remembered how fearfully Chantal had looked at him inside the chapel. He had initially thought that she somehow knew about his dream of Leslie. Then he had realized that he was not even confident it had been a dream. Deciphering if it had been a dream was hard enough; being told the entire vacation was a dream perplexed him to no end.

Earlier, when Andy's friends and family had left the room, the doctor had attempted to explain the accident. Andy could not even remember a severe thunderstorm, let alone a catastrophic tornado. At

88

the risk of sounding crazy, he had told the medical team that the last thing he remembered was being at Fallen Lake. He thought the bruise on his forehead would have been enough evidence to back up his story; Jon had wailed him with a tree branch. Everything about Fallen Lake remained vividly real to Andy. He could still smell the musty scent of the secret passages. Nevertheless, the doctors had insisted that Andy had only been dreaming.

Andy held his gaze on Chantal. He had so many questions that he wanted to ask her, but he was afraid of sounding like a lunatic. Did Leslie's grandparents' even have a house on Fallen Lake?

"Andy, they're going to keep you in the hospital for a few more days," his mother said as she pulled a chair up to his bed. "They're going to let me spend the night here."

Andy nodded, unsure of what to say. He wanted time to talk with Chantal privately, but he didn't know how to ask his family to leave. They seemed extremely worried about him. If he really had been in a coma for a month, and if there really had been a chance of him not surviving, then his family must have been devastated. If he had truly slept for a month, then what did that mean? Would he have to stay back a grade? Was he still Class President? Was Chantal still his girlfriend?

"Andy, I'm going to get a ride home from Robby," Chantal said. "My mom said I can miss school tomorrow and spend the day with you. Would you like that?"

Andy nodded intently.

"I love you," Chantal said and kissed him on the forehead. "God has answered many of my prayers today."

Andy smiled, wondering if any of her prayers had been for deliverance.

CHAPTER 19

Later that evening, after his mother fell asleep, Andy thought about his experience at Fallen Lake. He evaluated it first as a dream and then as a reality. No matter how hard he tried, he could not lean one way or the other. Although he had no idea what had been going on in his friends' lives—if he had indeed been in a coma—he was eager to compare the two worlds.

What boggled Andy's mind, no matter what way he looked at the situation, was how he could see the entire picture. While experiencing everything at the mansion, Andy had no idea what the others had been up to. As Andy sat in his hospital bed, memories had begun rushing through his mind. Oddly, they were not *his* memories.

Suddenly, he recalled seeing Chantal standing on the balcony and noticing Katherine in the woods. He remembered Lisa and Jon on the attic staircase, petrified by the blood. He could see Lisa and Bobby looking through books in the old library. He recalled the way Lisa's face had paled with anxiety. He saw Jon and Katherine searching through the attic for Chantal. Then he saw Chantal trapped inside of the dumbwaiter, crying out to God in prayer. Then he saw a blinding light—an angel. He could recite the angel's words. The scenario played through Andy's mind like a movie reel. His brain was being flooded with his friends' memories. *How can this be?*

While at the mansion, Andy had no idea what his friends were experiencing. He had not known where to find Chantal or that she had seen an angel. Why could he suddenly see the overall picture? Never had Andy dreamed something in first person and then been able to recall it in third person. What type of dream became clearer hours after it had been dreamt? Despite what the medical professionals had stated, Andy began to question the MRI results. How could a normally functioning brain redesign its memory?

As Andy continued to contemplate, the fear that weighed upon him grew heavier. How long would he be able to contest sleep? Where would he wake up next? Who would he wake up with? The line between reality and illusion in Andy's mind had been distorted beyond recognition. Andy glanced one last time at his sleeping mother before surrendering to slumber.

Part 2
The Enlightenment

Chapter 1

Friday morning, Chantal walked through the door of Andy's hospital room with the last two people Andy had expected to see: Chris Dunkin and Jason Davids. It took Andy a moment to remember that Chris had become his friend. Chris was no longer the loud, intoxicated, troublemaker that Andy had known of for years.

Andy swallowed deeply as he glanced at Jason. He began to wonder what Jason could possibly bring to the situation. *Why would he visit me? What prank does he have up his sleeve? What rumor does he want to spread around school?* Andy lowered his eyebrows and stared at Jason, wondering if his mind was playing tricks on him again; Jason looked sober, alert, and happy.

"Good morning!" Chantal cried out as she rushed to Andy's side. She leaned over and kissed him gently on the forehead. "I love you so much!"

"Hey, dude! How're you feeling?" Chris asked. He smiled as he shook Andy's hand. "Look at you, awake and healthy. What a miracle, huh?"

Andy nodded. "I'm feeling okay, but my thoughts are a little disoriented. I can't quite believe that I missed an entire month of my life."

"It's been quite a month," Jason spoke up and let out a deep breath.

"Chris and Jason organized a prayer service for you, right after your accident," Chantal said and glanced from Andy to the other boys. "Like half of Montgomery showed up. It was amazing."

"What?" Andy questioned her and glanced strangely from Jason to Chris. Nothing Chantal said made sense.

"Yeah, people really like you around here," Jason said and raised his eyebrows at Andy. "It only took about eight hours to gather thousands of people. You didn't wake up healthy by accident. People have been praying for you non-stop."

Andy swallowed. *This has to be another dream,* he thought. *Jason Davids? Talking to me about prayer? Okay, I'm not buying into this one. Leslie being psycho is more believable than this.*

"I came here to ask your forgiveness," Jason said and took a step closer to Andy's bed. "I'm sorry about what happened to you at the girls' house. Cathy and I were the ones who left Lady outside. I should have been the one to let her in. I hope you can forgive me for what happened to you."

Andy raised his eyebrows and stared at Jason, completely dumbfounded. A moment later he brought his hands to his head in frustration. *What world have I woken up in now?*

"Are you all right?" Chantal asked and leaned over him.

"I'm just overwhelmed," Andy replied after a few seconds. "Jay, I forgive you, but I don't even remember what happened. You guys planned a prayer service for me? Wow, I don't even know what to say. I wouldn't expect you to do that for me."

"Well, it wasn't just us," Chris said and shook his head. "A lot of people stepped up to help. You have a lot of fans."

Andy sighed in disbelief. "Wow," he said. "I guess I have a lot of catching up to do. I have to be honest; none of this seems real to me."

"None of us expected it to," Chantal said and smiled sympathetically. "God has done work around here while you were sleeping."

"What is that supposed to mean?" Andy asked.

Chantal glanced over at Jason and then back to Andy. "I don't want to overwhelm you any more than you already are," she replied. "It's all good stuff, but it's a story for another time."

"All right. I trust you," Andy said.

"Well, I think we should head to school," Chris spoke up and nodded toward the door. "It's good to see you, dude. It's great to have you back," he added and patted Andy on the shoulder.

"Thanks," Andy said, still finding the situation odd.

"We'll come visit you again," Jason said as he shook Andy's hand. "I'll probably come by later with Jessie and Pastor Mark."

Andy squinted at him in confusion.

"A story for another time," Jason added quickly. "See you later, guys."

"Bye," Chantal called.

"Why did Jason come here?" Andy asked Chantal the moment Chris and Jason left his room.

"I'm sure you have a lot of questions; that's why I'm going to spend the day here," Chantal replied, gazing at him warmly.

"I have more questions than you could even handle," Andy said, wondering if he was even talking to Chantal or just dreaming.

"I can't imagine how you must be feeling," Chantal said empathetically. "I'll try my best to explain everything."

"I don't think you can," Andy stated quickly.

"Why not?" Chantal asked with a confused look coating her face.

Andy sighed. "I don't know if I believe I was even in a coma. I don't even know if any of this is real. I don't know what I know!" he exclaimed in frustration.

"Then let's pray," Chantal suggested and took ahold of his hand.

"I don't feel like praying right now," Andy responded and pulled his hand away from Chantal.

Chantal glared at Andy. He couldn't tell if she was angry or just shocked. "God just delivered you from a coma, in good health, and you don't want to pray?!" she exclaimed.

"I think He's already done enough for me, so I probably shouldn't ask Him for anything else," Andy replied and grabbed Chantal's hand back.

"Andy, God wants to be involved in your life. He wants to bless you," Chantal said calmly. "How would you feel if you did something nice for me, and I stopped talking to you because of it?"

"That would be weird."

"Well, don't you think God feels the same way?"

Andy shrugged. "I guess. I don't know. Why do you always have to bring up God?"

"Because I love Him," Chantal replied defensively. "You can't say you love God if you don't like talking about Him. When you love someone, you enjoy talking about them."

Andy brought his hands to his forehead and closed his eyes. If what the angel had said to Chantal was true, then how could Andy pray to God? Clearly, God knew his heart was not in the right place. Chantal had never before questioned Andy's faith. Had an angel really visited her? Had his two worlds of memories somehow collided?

"Does Anderson like Katherine?" Andy asked suddenly as he dropped his hands to his sides.

Chantal appeared shocked by his question. "What does that have to do with anything?" Chantal asked.

"You said you would answer my questions. That isn't even a hard one, and you're already having issues." Andy rolled his eyes.

"Geez, I'm sorry! You just took me by surprise," Chantal replied. "Um, yeah there's been some talk about them liking each other. Last month, Katherine thought Bobby broke up with her, but it was just a misunderstanding."

Andy's stomach dropped.

"I think they like each other," Chantal said. "Why did you ask me that?"

"Would it be possible for me to ask you questions without having to explain my reasoning?" Andy asked and bit his bottom lip. "My thoughts are really disoriented, and I'm having trouble making sense of anything."

"Yeah, sure. I'm sorry," Chantal replied.

"How's Lisa?" Andy asked. "Did she handle what happened to me okay?"

"Well, she got a lot closer with Cathy," she said after a moment. "That's never a good thing."

"Has she been doing a lot of drugs?" Andy assumed.

Chantal shrugged. "I don't know her business."

"I worry about her," Andy said, suddenly feeling the urge to tell Chantal about Lisa's experience at the mansion.

"I do, too," Chantal said. "They pulled her up onto the Varsity Cheerleading Competition Squad. I hope that straightens her out. She said she had to quit smoking, so that's good."

"She stopped smoking weed?" Andy asked in astonishment.

Chantal shrugged. "I don't know, hopefully. I thought she meant cigarettes."

"Lisa doesn't smoke," Andy stated flatly. "It's actually her pet peeve."

Chantal shrugged. "Well, I've never seen her smoke, but she said she did. I don't know."

"She must have meant weed," Andy commented. "And if that's true, that's awesome. Jeff must be thrilled."

"Whatever," Chantal said with a long sigh. "Next question, please."

"All right, fine," Andy said, a bit taken back by Chantal's frustration. "Are you and Jon friends again?" he asked and tugged on her sweater.

Chantal frowned. "Yeah, we worked out our issues," she replied after a few seconds. "How did you know that?"

"Does he go to your church again?" Andy questioned her.

Chantal lowered her eyebrows and crossed her arms. "Andy, you're starting to freak me out," she said.

"So, he does, right?"

Chantal nodded.

"Wow, that is crazy."

"What is?"

Andy sighed. "I think I'm trapped between two worlds or something."

"Two worlds?" Chantal asked. "Well, you just came out of a coma, so you're probably going to have a hard time deciphering reality from illusion. That's why I suggested praying. God can make things clear to you."

Andy put his head down. "Chantal, I don't think God and I are on too good of terms," he admitted. "I'm not sure what I mean by that, but I have to figure some things out."

"Are you mad at Him because of your accident?" Chantal asked.

Andy shook his head from side to side. "Not at all," he replied and then took a deep breath. "I just need to figure out where my feet are planted."

Chantal's eyes grew wide.

"What?" Andy asked.

"Nothing," Chantal said and smiled oddly. "You just reminded me of something… that's all."

Andy eyed Chantal admiringly, wondering again if he should tell her about Fallen Lake. She'd be devastated to hear about his dream with Leslie. Could he leave that part out? The last thing he wanted was to upset Chantal. He would never hook up with Leslie, even if he were single.

Leslie was the socially "perfect" girl of his grade. Everyone loved her. She was the friendliest person Andy had ever met. He couldn't understand why she had acted so strangely at Fallen Lake. Then again, he had acted just as out of character: testy, jealous, and angry. *Maybe everything that happened in the mansion was a dream after all?*

"Leslie and Lisa are getting along okay, right?" Andy asked.

"I think so," Chantal replied. "Katherine's been a little distant from them, but I think they're all getting along fine."

"That's good," Andy said. "Adam and Leslie are still together?"

Chantal nodded.

"That's good, too," Andy said.

"Cathy and Jason broke up!" Chantal blurted out. "I've been dying to tell you, but I didn't want to overwhelm you."

Andy laughed. "What? Those two idiots? That would never happen."

"It did!" Chantal exclaimed with a laugh. "I'm serious. I saw your expression when Jason mentioned God. He became a Christian."

Andy cocked his head to the side. "What-huh-wait, what?" he stuttered.

Chantal nodded. "When you got hurt, Jason felt responsible," she said. "He was a mess about the whole thing and sought out Chris for advice. That's how they became friends again. One thing led to another, and it's a really long story, but a lot of good has come from your accident."

"That's crazy," Andy commented distractedly, again wondering if this could really be his life. If only he could remember the storm, then perhaps he would believe he had really been in a coma. The last thing he remembered before waking up inside the mansion was… hmmm… he couldn't remember.

"Chantal, could you walk me through what happened the day of the storm?" Andy asked.

"Of course," Chantal agreed.

She spent the next ten minutes explaining in detail what had happened on that day. Nothing she described sounded familiar to Andy.

"Have you ever heard of Fallen Lake?" Andy asked hesitantly.

"I've heard of it, but I've never been there," Chantal replied. "Why?"

Andy sighed and turned away from her.

"Is that where your dream took place?" Chantal asked and placed her hand on Andy's arm.

Andy turned and faced Chantal. "I don't know. I don't know what I know," he replied, sounding more frustrated than he meant to. "I'm afraid that if I fall asleep, I'll wake up in a whole different world. This has happened to me a couple of times. The only good thing is that you've been there every time."

Chantal smiled. "If you want to sleep, I'll be right here when you wake up."

"I *am* tired," Andy admitted. "Can you fit on the bed with me? You can lay down and watch a movie while I sleep."

"It's okay… I can just stay in the chair," Chantal stammered. "I'll be fine."

"Fair enough," Andy replied and smiled at his girlfriend. Chantal had always been a calming influence in his life. Just being around her made Andy's anxiety wane. He hoped that she would never look at him the way she had while she was climbing out of the dumbwaiter. All of the positive changes Andy had made to his lifestyle over the past two years had been a result of Chantal's influence. He believed that if he had not fallen in love with her in seventh grade, he probably would have become as much of a delinquent as Jason.

His uncanny ability to read people and perceive what they wanted to hear had granted Andy the talent of charming a crowd. For years, he had used his charm to get exactly what he wanted from everyone around him. While he had placed his manipulative tendencies on the shelf when he began dating Chantal, he often found himself acting the way the people around him wanted him to act. He was a unifier around Leslie, a party-buddy with Lisa, a sports fanatic around Bobby, an instigator alongside Jeff, and a Christian around Chantal. Andy had thought that his friends just brought out different parts of his character, but he was beginning to wonder if he even had a true personality. Had he really acted out of character in the mansion or was that his actual character? As he lay in his hospital bed with his eyes shut, he realized that he had very little conviction of his own. Was it amnesia or did he really not know himself?

Chapter 2

***

Three weeks later, Andy returned to school. He had stayed in the hospital for a week after awakening, compliments of Mayor Angeletti. Many of Andy's classmates had made their faces familiar around the hospital. Even some of his older brother's friends had visited, including Marc Dunkin, Michelle Taylor, and John Kelly. Andy could not believe the amount of attention he had received. His hospital room had overflowed with flowers, balloons, edible fruit arrangements, and greeting cards.

Andy's teachers had been gracious with him, allowing him to finish the term on schedule. Both his parents and teachers were impressed by how quickly Andy had been able to focus on schoolwork. During his two weeks at home after leaving the hospital, Andy had completed a month's worth of assignments.

Focusing on schoolwork had kept his mind off the haunting thoughts of demons, angels, and nightmares. Andy's memories of Fallen Lake had begun slipping away, much to his liking. He had mentioned the events of Fallen Lake to no one—not even Chantal. It had been easier for him to dismiss the adventure as a dream than to deal with the repercussions of it.

That morning, when Andy reached his locker, he stared blankly at it, realizing he would have to unlock it. The combination escaped his memory, and he dreaded the thought of asking the office for assistance.

"Hey!" Chantal exclaimed brightly as she appeared beside him. "Are you excited to be back?"

Andy bit his bottom lip and turned toward her. "What's my combination?" he whispered and gazed at her expectantly.

"You're lucky I know these things," Chantal sang and playfully nudged him aside. She turned the lock and slid open the latch with ease. "Twenty-seven, eight, twenty-eight," she said as she placed the lock in his hand.

"Thanks," Andy replied. He widened his eyes as he glanced inside his locker. It was lined with greeting cards, posters, and pictures. "Who did this?" he asked.

Chantal laughed. "Lisa and I did it last week. Everyone kept sliding cards into your locker and telling us about it, so we figured we'd make it look pretty for you," she explained.

Andy smiled. "Thank you so much! I'll have to read these after school. There are so many."

Andy felt someone tap on his shoulder. "Hi!" Lisa cried out as Andy turned around to face her.

"Hey!" Andy exclaimed, immediately throwing his arms around her. "Thank you so much for helping Chantal with my locker."

Lisa laughed and pulled free from their embrace. "It was the least I could do. Hi, Tal."

"Hey," Chantal greeted her. "Lisa did more than help me; it was her idea."

"Oh, details," Lisa said as she shrugged and smiled warmly. "I bet every one of your classes is going to have a party for you today. I know we're having breakfast for you in history."

"Really? Sweet!" Andy cried. "That's what I'm talking about!"

"Rosetti!" Leslie called out as she rushed toward him. She threw her arms around him and jumped up and down. "I'm so happy you're back! We're nothing without our president!"

Andy laughed and quickly pulled free from her embrace. Being in her arms just felt wrong. "Hey, dude. What's up?" he greeted Adam Case, Leslie's boyfriend, who was standing to her right. "It's so good to see you guys without being tied to a hospital bed."

"Did you catch up on a lot of work during your two weeks of isolation?" Adam asked. "I bet you'll be pulling off A's by the end of the term."

Andy shrugged and flipped open his arms. "I'll do my best."

"You better have gotten a lot done," Leslie stated in an amused matter. "We're not friends with people who turn us away for Xbox marathons."

Andy smiled. "All right, you caught me. I blew off my schoolwork and ditched you guys for *Call of Duty*."

"There he is!" Jeff Brooke shouted from down the hall, cupping his mouth so that his normally loud voice was amplified. "Give Rosetti a warm welcome back!" he called out, while clapping his hands together loudly.

Bobby walked beside Jeff, rolling his eyes. Within seconds everyone in the crowded locker hall began clapping and cheering for Andy.

"I'm going to kill your boyfriend," Andy said as he nudged Lisa. "Thanks, guys," he said loudly and waved his hand in the air for a split second.

"Dude, Rosetti, you look like hell. What happened? Did you have a rough month or something?" Jeff teased Andy and punched him in the arm as soon as he reached his locker.

"You're an @#%," Andy said and playfully pushed Jeff into the row of lockers.

"What's up?" Bobby greeted Andy with a slight nod.

"Hey, guy! Give me a hug!" Andy exclaimed and threw his arms out in the air. "We heart hugs not drugs!" he sang and patted his best friend on the back.

"Good to see you're back to your old self," Bobby said and pushed Andy off of him.

"Andy, I have to go to homeroom," Chantal said as she grabbed ahold of his arm.

"Oh, all right," Andy said. "See ya in history."

"Right," Chantal replied, smiling slightly. "I'll see you guys later," she said to the group before walking off toward her homeroom.

"So, are we going to party it up big or what?" Jeff asked, once Chantal was out of hearing distance. "It's not every day one of your best friends returns from a coma land."

Andy laughed. "Yeah, I think a party could be in the cards."

"My parents said we could have a party for you at my house in New Hampshire," Leslie spoke up, smiling with excitement. "They said we could invite anyone we want."

"Really? That's sick!" Andy cried. "I'd love that. Are you near any ski resorts?"

"Hey, slow down, buddy. Do you think it's safe to be on skis already?" Lisa asked, eyeing him warily.

"Probably not," Andy said with a shrug, "but I'm game for whatever."

"Cool. Well, think of people you'd want to invite. I have to get to homeroom," Leslie said. "Come on, Adam. Bye, guys! Love you all!"

"Bye, Lee," Andy, Lisa, Jeff, and Bobby called in unison.

"She's so funny," Andy commented. "Any excuse to throw a party, right?"

"You know it," Jeff said. "Lis, you have to check your cheering schedule. We might have to go up over Christmas break."

Lisa nodded.

"Oh, yeah, how's cheering going?" Andy asked. "I heard they pulled you up to varsity for competition."

Lisa smiled. "I like it a lot. It's going really well. I get to practice with Kat and cheer at games with Lee, so it's the best of both worlds."

"Nice," Andy said. "I can't wait to come to a game. They don't let you cheer at the varsity games?"

"I did for the Thanksgiving game because we did some of our competition stunts at halftime," Lisa replied. "Ally said they might need me for basketball cheering in the winter."

"That'd be awesome," Andy said. "It makes me happy to see you so happy."

"Oh, isn't that touching," Jeff sang sarcastically.

Lisa punched her boyfriend lightly in the stomach. "He can be happy for me, jerk," she said. "Let's walk Andy to homeroom."

"Guys, I'm not a wounded puppy," Andy stated with a smirk. "I think Bobby can get me there okay. We happen to share a homeroom."

"All right, see ya in history," Lisa sang and patted Andy on the shoulder as she walked past him.

"Later," Jeff called as he placed his hands on Lisa's tiny waste.

"So, what? You can walk by yourself or something? You're allowed to do that? Or did you bring a leash to school?" Bobby asked dryly.

"Actually, a leash brought me to school," Andy laughed as he shut his locker. "Homeroom. Wow. I haven't walked through that door in almost two months. That's craziness right there."

"Yeah, I'm sure Katherine will be excited to see you," Bobby said.

"Oh, yeah. Why didn't she come to my locker?" Andy asked as he and Bobby turned the corner to the freshmen class hallway.

Bobby sighed. "Probably because I was there."

"Are you guys fighting, again?" Andy questioned him.

Bobby shrugged. "I don't know. Things are weird. I don't need to elaborate; you'll see for yourself."

Chantal took her seat in homeroom and immediately rested her head on her desk. She was drained of energy, emotion, tears, and positive thoughts. She had spent six out of the past seven weeks without Andy. During that time, she had spent hours each day reading the Bible, feeding her spirit with God's Word. She was amazed by how clearly God had spoken to her. She would pray for guidance, open up to a random page, and read the answer to her prayer. Whether it was a parable given by Jesus or an Old Testament event that related to her issue, God had led Chantal to His answers to her prayers each day.

A heavy burden had been laid on Chantal's heart. She realized after weeks of prayer that its heaviness was a result of her lack of faith and reluctance to die to self. She had studied the Bible enough to know that those who try to save their life will lose it, and those who surrender to God's guidance will find fulfillment, blessings, and peace. In other words, Chantal was learning the importance of putting God's desires for her life before her own. By holding on tightly to what God was asking her to let go, Chantal was only making the process more painful.

"What is wrong with you?" her twin sister Cathy asked, sounding more concerned than annoyed for once.

Chantal lifted her head off the desk. "Nothing, I'm just tired," she replied. "I was up late, talking to Jon."

"Now that your boyfriend is back from the dead, don't you think you should lay off the late-night phone conversations with Jon?" Cathy asked.

"It's not like Andy would stay up late talking to me," Chantal said and rolled her eyes. "It's not like we can even talk on the same level," she added beneath her breath.

Cathy lowered her eyebrows and eyed Chantal warily. She opened her mouth, looking as if she wanted to say something, but then quickly shut it.

"What?" Chantal asked.

"Nothing. Forget it," Cathy replied and put her head down.

"Just say it," Chantal pressed her. "Please?"

Cathy looked up at her. Chantal thought she looked nervous.

"It's just that, well, this is awful to even say, but you seemed a lot happier when Andy was in a coma," Cathy admitted slowly.

Chantal widened her eyes and stared at Cathy in disbelief.

Cathy began shaking her head. "I don't mean that you were happy that he was in a coma. I don't mean that at all. But I don't know how else to word what I'm trying to say."

Chantal swallowed the large lump in her throat and turned away from her sister. A moment later, she rested her head in her hands, wishing that she could sleep the day away.

<hr>

Andy walked into homeroom with Bobby right as the bell began ringing. Immediately, his classmates began clapping and cheering for him. Andy felt his face flush as he smiled back at everyone.

"Thanks, guys. That means a lot," Andy said as he walked across the room and took his assigned seat between Katherine and Jessie Robins.

"It's so good to see you!" Katherine cried as she threw her arms around him. "You should have seen how lost we were at last month's student council meeting. Clearly, you're president for a reason."

"Ha. I'm sure you guys were fine," Andy replied and pulled free from her embrace. "How's everything going?"

"Good," Katherine said and nodded intently.

"Well, that's good," Andy said and glanced over at Bobby. "Are you and Bobby going to come over Wednesday night for dinner? My mom's having a little thing for me."

"Oh, really?" Katherine asked. "That would be fun."

"I'm just going to invite Chantal, you, Bobby, Lisa, Jeff, Lee, and Adam," Andy said. "I want to keep it to my best friends, even though there's a lot of other people I wouldn't mind coming. I just don't want to overload my mom."

"That makes sense," Katherine said. "I'm sure everyone else would understand. Chris, Jason, and Jon go to church on Wednesday nights anyway."

"Oh, that's right. Chantal does, too," Andy recalled and bit his bottom lip. "I'm sure she could skip a week for my sake. That's so funny that Jason goes to church now. I bet he's taking so much heat for it."

"You'd be surprised," Katherine said with an amused smile. "The only reason Chris got harassed so much was because of Jason. Jason's clearly not going to harass himself."

"Are you kidding me? The class punk pulled a one-eighty, and everyone's fine with it?" Andy asked in disbelief.

"Yeah. It's one less jerk to worry about ruining your day," Katherine replied matter-of-factly. "I'm not going to complain about that. Are you?"

"No, but that's a really bold move. I never thought he had it in him," Andy admitted, finding himself bothered by Jason's apparent conversion.

CHAPTER 3

Chantal hurried into her first-period history class, hoping that she had beat Andy there. Jon, Chris, and Bryan were already sitting in the back row. Since Bryan and Andy were in the same homeroom, Chantal assumed Andy must have gotten held up in the hallway by his many admirers. Sighing, she dropped her books onto the desk in front of Jon.

"How's it going?" Jon asked.

Chantal took her seat and then turned to face him. Jon cocked his head to the side and gazed at her sympathetically.

A moment later, Andy walked into the classroom with Lisa and Leslie. He immediately glanced at Chantal and Jon. As he did, Chantal felt a pang of guilt. She was not happy to see him, and she felt horrible about it.

"Hey, guys," Andy said as he sat down beside Chantal. "Wow, it's so weird being back here. The last time I was here, we were all talking about midterm grades and how Bobby was acting weird…oh, wow… I remember that. That's weird. How come I can remember that but not the tornado later that day?"

"Trauma," Chantal said. "That's what happens."

"Andy, Jeff had a good point about my cheering schedule," Lisa spoke up from her seat behind Andy and beside Jon. "I was just talking to Leslie, and we'll probably have to go to New Hampshire over Christmas vacation."

Andy turned to Lisa. "Whatever works best for you guys," he said.

"We can go ice skating on the lake, and I bet my dad will let us use the snowmobiles!" Leslie exclaimed enthusiastically.

"That sounds awesome," Andy said. "I can't believe everyone is doing so many nice things for me. That's so kind of your parents, Lee."

"Well, they knew how downhearted I was when you were in the hospital, so they offered it to cheer me up," Leslie replied. "It gave me something to look forward to and kept me in the mind-set that you were going to wake up."

"Very cool," Andy stated. "Works for me."

"Who are you going to invite?" Lisa asked.

"How many people can fit in your house, Lee?" Andy asked.

Leslie shrugged. "My parents can drive up twelve people. People can sleep on couches if they have to, but we have four bedrooms."

"The girls can have first dibs on the bedrooms," Andy said. "The guys will be fine on couches."

"I already told my parents that you would probably invite Adam, Jeff, and Bobby," Leslie said. "I wasn't sure who else you'd invite for guys."

Chantal listened, realizing that Leslie had put Andy on the spot in front of everyone. She hoped Andy would invite Jon, Chris, and Bryan.

"Well…you said twelve people…right? Two of them being your parents?" Andy stammered.

Leslie nodded.

"Obviously me, Jeff, Bobby, Adam, you, Chantal, Lisa, and Katherine take eight of those spots," Andy rambled. "I don't know how to choose between Jon, Chris, Jay, Bryan, Court, and Marielle. They've all done a lot of nice things for me."

"Don't worry about me," Jon spoke up. "I understand if you're limited."

"Me either," Chris said. "My parents are taking me, Katie, and Marielle away skiing for the week at Killington."

"Wow, that's sick!" Andy cried. "You're lucky."

Chris nodded. "It'll be entertaining," he said. "Marielle's never put on a ski in her life."

"Jason and Courtney are probably going away with their rich families," Lisa commented and raised her perfectly shaped eyebrows. "Don't they go away for every school vacation? Long weekends, too?" She laughed in a smug manner.

Chantal rolled her eyes, wondering if Lisa would ever realize that she has no legitimate reason for detesting Courtney.

"I'll just invite everyone and see who can come," Andy announced. "If rides end up being a problem, we'll figure something out."

"That's fine," Leslie agreed. "You should invite Alyssa, too, so she doesn't feel left out," she added.

Andy nodded. "Oh, yeah," he said and turned toward Chantal. "You guys are friends again. That's pretty cool."

Chantal smiled at him, wondering if he really approved of her and Alyssa's friendship or if he was merely trying to appear supportive.

"Okay, class! It's time to welcome Andy back," their teacher called out, grabbing everyone's attention. "Let's take the first twenty minutes of class to celebrate Andy's healthy return." A variety of juices, bagels, muffins, donuts, and fresh fruit had been laid out on the front table while Chantal and her friends had been talking.

"Who paid for all this?" Andy blurted out, sounding astonished as he glanced at Chantal.

"We chipped in," Chantal replied.

"I have a good life," Andy stated. He let out a short laugh and smiled at Chantal. He looked like he was expecting a response from her. She arched her lips into a small smile before quickly turning away from him.

CHAPTER 4

Andy stared at Chantal in disbelief as they exited their history classroom. A simple invitation to dinner with his family had turned into an argument—something he had never expected.

"Andy!" Chantal cried. "How could you just expect me to miss church?"

"Oh my gosh! You go to church, like, five days a week! I figured you could miss one night to have dinner with my family," Andy replied defensively as he and Chantal pushed their way through the crowded hall.

Chantal sighed. "I don't think I can go to your dinner," she said angrily. "I was hoping you would come to church with me on Wednesday. I'm disappointed that you won't be there. Everyone prayed for you around the clock. The least you could do is come to Bible study. Do you not appreciate what everyone there did for you? Don't you get it?"

Andy stopped in the middle of the hallway and faced Chantal. "You are unbelievable. Do I mean nothing to you all of a sudden? It is just one night! It's the night that works best for my parents. I can go to church with you on Sunday."

Chantal's green eyes filled with tears. Before one tear could plunge onto her face, she silently pushed past Andy. Andy turned to watch Chantal make her way through the sea of freshmen. *How can she be mad at me for inviting her to dinner at my house? She's acting like I broke plans with her, but she never asked me to go to Bible study! Why does everyone else seem happier to see me than her?* As many questions ran through Andy's mind, he felt anger rising up inside of him. *What are my parents going to think when Chantal doesn't show up for dinner? You would think after I almost died last month that she would jump at the chance to spend time with me! This makes no sense.*

"What was that about?" Lisa asked as she appeared beside Andy with Leslie, Adam, and Bobby.

"Oh, Chantal is pissed because my dinner party is the same night as Bible study," Andy replied, hearing the anger in his tone.

"That's crazy!" Leslie exclaimed. "I'm sorry, but if my boyfriend had been in a coma for a month, I wouldn't leave his side for anything."

"She's going to realize that she's being irrational, dude," Adam said and patted Andy on the shoulder. "She's been through a lot this month. Give her a break."

"She had more faith than all of us that you were going to pull through," Bobby stated. "She was really strong. If God got her through that, then she probably doesn't feel right about skipping church. She's your girlfriend, but I know her pretty well, and I don't think she's trying to hurt you."

"No way! Chantal would never intentionally hurt anyone," Lisa chimed in while shaking her head from side to side. "I saw her run off in tears. She's obviously the one hurting. You should be talking this out with her right now—not us."

"What? Do you guys all love Chantal now or something?" Andy questioned his friends as he angrily threw his arms up in the air.

"It's not about that," Lisa replied immediately. "Obviously, we're more your friends than hers. I just think we can sympathize with her because we know what she went through while you were in a coma."

Andy rolled his eyes and shook his head. "Too bad you guys don't know what I went through in a coma," he retorted. "I'll see you later," he added and stormed away from his friends.

⁂

"Remember what I told you last night?" Chantal asked as she stared, teary eyed, up at Jon. She was leaning against the row of lockers outside of her science classroom. "What we prayed about?"

111

Jon nodded. His dark brown eyes were filled with deep concern.

"I got confirmation," Chantal said. "So quickly. I can't believe it."

Jon cocked his head to the side. "That just shows you how much God loves you."

Chantal dropped her eyes to the floor and nodded. She felt a line of tears stream down her left cheek. Confirmation that God was not Andy's top priority was the last thing Chantal had wanted.

Chantal felt Jon's hand on her shoulder. She looked up at him, helplessly.

"Tal, you can't go into class upset like this," Jon said. "No matter what happens, you know that everything is working together for good. Don't cry. Think of what the Apostle Paul went through or what Christ endured. People always say that they would give up their lives for their God, and I know you are one of those people. This is just one part of your life He is asking you to give up and look at you; you're a mess. If God's telling you to break up with Andy, He has a reason."

Chantal could not find any words to speak. She dropped her eyes to the floor and stared at Jon's shell-toe sneakers.

"You know the playground metaphor that you like to tell?" Jon asked. "Your Father is trying to take you to Disney World right now, but you're holding onto the monkey bars for dear life. You've got tears streaming down your face, and your Father is trying to take your hand, but you won't let him because you won't loosen your grip off the rusty monkey bars. He knows best Chantal."

He's right, she thought. *He's one-hundred percent right.* Chantal glanced up at Jon and began wiping tears off her face. She nodded slightly, patted his shoulder, and then ducked into her classroom without uttering another word.

Thirty seconds later, Andy entered the classroom and slumped into the seat beside Chantal. "I'm sorry," he muttered.

Chantal stared blankly at her pink fingernails, pretending that she had not noticed him.

"I'll see if my mom can change the dinner to Thursday," Andy said. "If she can, then I'll come to church with you on Wednesday. Okay?"

Chantal looked over at him.

"I've been acting kind of selfish lately," Andy said quietly. "I think I've gotten used to everyone dropping everything for me. Thanks for putting me in my place."

Chantal crossed her arms.

"I mean, the school system bent the rules for me; Leslie's parents are taking us away; you and Lisa decorated my locker; my classes are throwing parties for me; my mom is having a dinner for me; I've gotten hundreds of cards and presents; I think I'm becoming spoiled," Andy rambled, while gazing at Chantal like a scolded puppy.

"Andy, you—"

"—Good morning, class! Let's all welcome back Andy before we begin!" their science teacher called out loudly.

Immediately, a fake smile appeared on Andy's face. Chantal scowled.

"The class has a present for you, Andy," their teacher said.

Andy glanced quickly at Chantal as he stood up. She raised her eyebrows at him and shrugged, unable to mirror his forged expression.

<h1 style="text-align:center">CHAPTER 5</h1>

After the bell rang, Katherine and Jason left their Latin classroom together, engaged in playful conversation. "So, how lucky do you feel to have three classes in a row with me?" Jason asked. "I bet your dying for a new schedule, huh?"

"Oh, I can't get rid of you that easily!" Katherine teased him. "If anything, we'll end up in more of the same classes next term. Obviously, you signed up for fashion design with me. I can tell that's your calling."

Jason nudged Katherine playfully. "You're a real piece of work, Rossi. I don't know why everyone thinks you're so sweet. The abuse I take from you is unreal. No wonder Bob's so tough on the field. He's got you to go home to: a drill sergeant in disguise. That pearl necklace doesn't fool me."

"Your sarcasm doesn't fool me," Katherine retorted. "You've lost your sting. People aren't afraid of you anymore. Without the fear content working for ya, I'm afraid you're going to have to pretend to be charming. How's that charisma thing working out? Got any yet?"

"I think I've pulled you out of your shell," Jason said and draped his arm around Katherine's shoulders.

"I thought we jumped out of the boat together," Katherine said as she paused at her locker.

114

Jason rolled his light blue eyes. "Oh, yeah. That's right. Good stuff, Kat. I have to grab my binder. See ya next class."

"See ya," Katherine called.

"You two are awfully friendly," Bobby said as he suddenly appeared beside Katherine.

Katherine's heart began pounding at the sound of his voice. "Oh, please, Bobby!" she said in disgust. "What girl isn't Jay friendly with?" She unlocked her locker without glancing in her boyfriend's direction.

"He's a single boy on the prowl," Bobby said dryly.

Katherine looked over at Bobby and rolled her eyes. "You need to stop doing that."

"What?" Bobby asked defensively. "It's true. Jay's a ladies' man. He's always been one."

Katherine sighed. "Not that," she said as she placed her Latin book on the top shelf of her locker. "Stop implying that I like every guy I talk to."

"I'm not trying to pick a fight with you, but it's not just me who thinks you're acting weird," Bobby said. "It's strange to see you hanging out with Chantal and Jessie more than Lisa and Leslie. You didn't even come to Andy's locker this morning, and now you're all buddy-buddy with Jason Davids. Do you know how that looks?"

You are such a snob, she thought. "I knew I would see Andy in homeroom," she replied. "Sorry if I missed the locker memo. My bad," she added and slammed her locker shut.

"Do you even like me anymore? Seriously? Or am I just an annoyance to you?" Bobby questioned Katherine. He stepped in front of her before she could walk away from her locker.

Katherine glared up at him angrily. "It's not the time and definitely not the place for this conversation," she replied as she pushed past him.

"What is *that* supposed to mean?" Bobby called out and grabbed hold of her arm.

Katherine reluctantly stopped and turned to face him. "I can't be fake anymore. There's something missing from my life, and I need to figure out what. I can't try to fill it with you. I can't hide behind Lis and Lee anymore. I need to find myself. You need to let me do that, by either sticking it out or letting me go!" she exclaimed as she felt tears begin welling up inside her eyes.

Bobby stared at Katherine with a look of great confusion.

"I can't talk about this stuff in school!" Katherine cried.

"I didn't realize there was a problem, Kat," Bobby said. "The last thing I wanted to do was upset you."

"Then stop throwing accusations at me and listen to what I say on the phone every night," Katherine stated sternly. "I've been trying to tell you this for weeks, and you just don't get it. I have to go to class now. We can talk later."

"Kat, are we okay?" Bobby asked.

Katherine recognized the fearful look in Bobby's eyes. She sighed and looked down at the ground.

"You still love me, don't you?" Bobby asked.

Katherine nodded slightly and bit her bottom lip. "I'll see you at lunch, okay?"

"Hug me," Bobby whined. He threw his arms around her and squeezed her tightly.

Chapter 6

Butterflies fluttered around Cathy's stomach as she and Marc Dunkin walked to the cafeteria. Her heart raced with excitement after each word he spoke.

"Do you have any big plans for Christmas break?" Marc asked.

Cathy shrugged. "I haven't really thought that far ahead. You?"

"Well, some of the crew rented a condo at Loon for the week, so I might go up for a few nights," Marc replied. "I didn't want to commit myself to the entire week. You never know what opportunities may arise."

"Who's going?" Cathy asked.

"I think Katie, Robby, Ally, Matt, John, Day, Michelle, Samson, and Bob-o," Marc said. "Luke, Laurelle, Missy, and Pat are sticking around here."

"That's a pretty clean divide," Cathy said. "You and Luke won't find it hard to get into trouble around here."

"Luke never does," Marc said with a laugh. "I'm this close to convincing Katie to give you a copy of her ID."

Cathy widened her eyes. "For real?" she asked. "She'd do that?"

Marc nodded. "Katie's pretty chill like that," he replied. "Besides, how else am I supposed to take you out in Boston?"

Cathy gazed at Marc skeptically. "What about Julianna?" she questioned him, referring to her close friend whom Marc had kissed at a party a couple of months prior.

"She could probably ask Jess or Rachel," Marc replied carelessly.

Cathy smiled. *Maybe he likes me more than her,* she thought. "I'd love to go out with you in Boston," she admitted.

"If I went to Loon for New Years, would you want to come?" Marc asked as he held open the cafeteria door for her.

Cathy dropped her jaw. Her heart pounded. Excitement jolted her veins. "I might be able to get permission," she replied.

"Since when do *you* ask for permission?" Marc teased her.

Cathy smiled. "I'm trying to be more honest with my parents," she said. "When I was going out with Jason, I hid so many things from them. I feel bad about it now."

Marc lowered his eyebrows and smiled. His blue eyes twinkled in an adoring manner. "Then let me know what they say," he said.

Cathy nodded. "Well, I'm going to sit with Lisa and Julianna, but I'll see you later."

"Later," Marc called and headed off toward the seniors' side of the cafeteria.

"So, you're not going away with everyone to Leslie's cottage?" Katherine asked as she walked with Jon toward their lunch table. She glanced around, wondering if Bobby had reached the cafeteria yet. She knew that the sight of her and Jon would infuriate him. She did not care at all.

"No, I'm not Andy's favorite person," Jon replied. "He seems to think that I still like Chantal."

"A lot of people think that," Katherine said quietly.

"Chantal and I are friends because we can relate to each other and we trust each other. We both know where we stand in our friendship. I wish everyone else would stop making something out of it that it isn't," Jon stated, sounding annoyed.

"Well, you guys are always together, so that fuels the gossip," Katherine said.

"She's one of my best friends. I'm not going to stop hanging out with her because people are judgmental," Jon retorted. "You should know by now where my interest lies."

Katherine felt her cheeks redden as she glanced up at Jon.

Andy walked into the cafeteria, deep in thought. He spotted Chantal sitting at a table with Alyssa, Jon, Katherine, Courtney, Bryan, Chris, Marielle, Jason, and Jessie. Leslie, Adam, Lisa, Jeff, Cathy, and Julianna were sitting at the next table over. *This is weird*, he thought. *Jessie Robins talking to Alyssa Kelly? Cathy Kagelli sitting with Julianna Camen? Katherine **not** sitting between Lisa and Leslie? And where is Bobby? Is he going to sit with his girlfriend or with his friends?*

Andy suddenly realized that he had to make the same choice. Was he going to sit with Chantal or with his best friends? Had Chantal even saved him a seat? Would he be welcomed at her table? Did everyone know about their fight? *Asking Chantal to skip church probably sounded like murder to Jessie Robins*, Andy reasoned.

Chantal let out a heavy sigh as Andy neared her table. As she watched him make his way across the cafeteria, she admired his beauty. Andy possessed everything any normal high school girl would want in a boyfriend. From a worldly standpoint, he had it all.

Letting Andy go was simultaneously the last thing and only thing that she wanted to do. Chantal realized that Andy was number one in her heart, and that was a problem. She knew that God should be number one. Putting Andy first was hindering her spiritual growth. Chantal wanted God to use her for His purposes, so that she could become the best version of herself.

In eighth grade, Andy had swept Chantal off her feet. She had been heartbroken over her breakup with Jon and, therefore, very vulnerable. Losing Andy to a coma had taught Chantal a lot about her own heart and desires. It was not until she only had God to cling to that she realized He was all she ever needed. Chantal sighed, wishing that Andy would desire to grow closer to God.

One year prior, when Andy was volunteering at a homeless shelter, Chris had shown up with his cousin Taylor. By the way Taylor interacted with some of the inhabitants, Andy assumed he was there to deal drugs. That was when Chantal began praying heavily for Chris's salvation. Sitting at her lunch table and glancing over at Chris, Chantal was immediately reminded of the Cross. *How can I question God's will for my life after seeing Him so miraculously answer my prayers for Chris?*

Additionally, she had prayed for two years for Jon to return to his faith—an answered prayer. She had prayed for her friendship with Alyssa to be restored since their seventh-grade fallout—another answered prayer. Chantal was so happy that she had persevered in prayer, even when it had seemed like God was not listening. He had answered her prayers in His perfect timing and worked everything out better than she had ever imagined.

She glanced again at Andy and sighed. For whatever reason—one she did not need to understand—it was her time to be single. She had to take God's hand, even though that meant letting go of the monkey bars and leaving her favorite playground.

CHAPTER 7

Wednesday night, Andy looked around his dining-room table and then hung his head. As a result of everyone's conflicting schedules, Andy had been unable to switch the night of his dinner. That left him with six of his best friends, a five-course meal, and a girlfriend he could not get ahold of.

"Thank you for inviting us over, Mr. and Mrs. Rosetti," Leslie said with a gleaming smile.

"Yeah, thanks!" Lisa cried.

"Thank you," Katherine, Adam, Bobby, and Jeff said in unison.

"Honestly, it's our pleasure," Mrs. Rosetti replied. "We're so happy that Andy has such good friends."

"We enjoy any opportunity to see Andy happy," Mr. Rosetti added as he nodded toward Andy.

Andy rolled his eyes. "You keep spoiling me," he said appreciatively, hoping that no one noticed the sadness in his eyes.

"Have you decided who you want to invite to my lake house?" Leslie asked.

"I think it's going to be us, Chantal, Alyssa, and Jon," Andy replied.

Katherine's head shot up immediately. Andy pretended not to notice how flush her face grew and how nauseated Bobby looked at the mention of Jon's name.

"Chris, Bryan, Courtney, and Marielle are all going away for Christmas break," Andy continued. "Jason said he wanted to stay home with his brother. I didn't invite Cathy, Julianna, or Jessie because they're not really my friends. Alyssa and Jon were there for Chantal when I was in a coma, and I appreciate that a lot. I'm glad they're coming."

"I love them both!" Leslie exclaimed. "This is going to be so much fun."

Lisa sent a sympathetic smile in Andy's direction. "Chantal must be happy that her two best friends are coming," she said.

"I hope so," Andy said downheartedly.

Andy's mother glanced at him. He could read her eyes. She clearly had noticed the sadness in his tone. "It's too bad that she couldn't be here," she said. "I thought she might have come over before church."

"I don't think she had a ride," Andy stated. "She would be here if she did."

"That's too bad," Mr. Rosetti said. "If I had known, I would have driven her to church. She's really devoted, huh?"

"Yeah," Andy, Lisa, and Bobby stressed in unison.

"That's good, Andy," Mrs. Rosetti said. "I've always hoped you would marry a girl with strong morals."

"Do you think Robby and Michelle Taylor will ever get back together?" Katherine asked, glancing from Andy to Mrs. Rosetti. "I've gotten to know Michelle through cheerleading, and she is amazing! She's full of faith and good morals."

Jeff looked at Andy and dropped his jaw. "Your brother dated *Michelle Taylor?*" he asked.

Andy laughed. "Yeah, in eighth grade," he replied.

"Which one is Michelle?" Mrs. Rosetti asked and turned toward her husband.

"I think she's the one who beat him for Vice President in tenth grade," Mr. Rosetti replied.

Andy shook his head. "I don't know about that, but she's the pretty one."

"Ohhhh," Mr. and Mrs. Rosetti sang in unison.

Lisa rolled her eyes. "That poor girl. People only know her by her beauty. It doesn't seem to matter that she's Homecoming Queen, Student Body Treasurer, Co-captain of the varsity cheerleading squad, Captain of the ski team, and a wicked nice person," she rambled.

"Oh, yeah! Poor Michelle! It must *stink* to be gorgeous," Leslie said sarcastically. "I'm sure you'd know all about that, Lis."

Lisa blushed. "Stop," she said. "There's a lot more value to people than their physical appearance, and I just wish *some people* would take note of that."

Andy glanced at Lisa strangely. That was one of the last things he expected to hear come from her mouth. He cocked his head to the side, wondering if she was finally softening up.

⁂

Chantal ran up to Chris as Bible study was letting out. "Can I talk to you for a minute?" she asked as she grabbed ahold of his arm and looked up at him pleadingly.

Chris's blue eyes filled with concern. "Yeah, Tal, of course," he replied. "What's going on?"

"Let's go sit in the auditorium," Chantal said. "My parents won't be done talking with everyone for an hour. Don't worry, though, I won't take up that much of your time."

"I have a nine o'clock meeting with Pastor Mark," Chris said. "You have my undivided attention until then."

Once they reached the auditorium, Chantal began confiding in Chris about everything that had been going on between her and God regarding Andy. "Did Pastor Mark ever talk to you about being unequally yoked?" she asked.

Chris stared at Chantal for a second before answering. "You know what? Let's pray about this before I say anything," he said.

You are so perfect, Chantal thought as she gazed at him respectfully.

"Dear Lord, I lift this conversation up to You, and I pray that you fill Chantal and me with Your Holy Spirit. Please give us wisdom and discernment. Please guide our conversation. Please drain me of my opinions and speak through me. Please give Chantal an open heart and open ears to hear everything You'd like her to know. I pray this in Jesus' name, Amen," Chris said.

Chantal smiled slightly. "Thanks," she said.

"Pastor Mark and I have talked about the dangers of being unequally yoked," Chris stated. "He was concerned because I claimed

123

that I wanted to find God's plan for my life but had a non-believing girlfriend. I knew that Marielle would start believing if she gave God the chance to reveal Himself to her. There's a lot that no one knows about my relationship with her…and I'm not going to expose it…but what I will say is that I let go of the idea that 'I had to be with her' and made myself open to whatever God had in mind. Soon after, she started showing an interest in developing a relationship with God. It was like when I let go of her in my heart, God got ahold of her. Maybe He was testing me to see if I was going to deem dating her more important than obeying Him. I just know that what I sacrificed is nothing compared to what He sacrificed for me."

"So, you didn't actually break up with her? You just let go of her emotionally?" Chantal asked.

Chris let out a short laugh. "Well, I wasn't going to tell you this because no one knows. Please don't mention this to Marielle," he said, sounding a bit hesitant. "Okay?"

Chantal nodded. "But you don't have to tell me. It's okay," she said.

"I trust you," he said. "It's fine. So, the day that I planned to tell her that we needed to break up until we could walk the same path, she came to me and said that she wanted to borrow my Bible."

Chills shot up Chantal's spine. "Really?" she asked and widened her eyes.

Chris laughed. "Yeah," he said, sounding amazed by the fact. His blue eyes sparkled as he smiled at her. "I couldn't believe it. She said that she wanted to learn about God so that she could recognize Him at work in her life."

"That's really cool," Chantal stated, remembering how happy she had been when Marielle agreed to go to church with her.

"So, I didn't end up breaking up with her because she stepped onto my path, and we've been walking together ever since," Chris said. "But I really, really, really thought I was going to have to break up with her. It was like how God asked Abraham to sacrifice Isaac, but then He provided the ram when He saw that Abraham was willing to obey Him. God didn't want Abraham to hurt Isaac. He wanted to see if Isaac was before Him in Abraham's heart."

Ouch, Chantal thought. *You just hit the nail on the head.*

"I know you love Andy; that's an inarguable fact," Chris continued. "If God's calling you to be single right now, then you can't assume a broken-up state would be permanent. You have no idea what

God's plans are for you and Andy. Maybe He's trying to get Andy's attention, and He's working through you. Maybe He is going to transform Andy into the spiritual leader you'll want to marry someday. God knows everything, and He knows what's best for both of you. Even though Andy doesn't always walk with integrity, he is still one of God's children. God loves him just as much as you. If He's asking you to break up with Andy, then it's in Andy's best interest, too. You should want what's best for Andy."

"Chris, sometimes I wonder if he really even believes in God!" Chantal blurted out. "I know that I can't judge if he does or not because only God knows his heart, but the Bible says to judge a tree by its fruit. I don't see any good fruit in his life. I *so* badly want to see it. I want to see that his faith is real. I want to know that he is not faking it just to be with me. I want him to want what you and I have. I really do want what's best for him."

Chris patted Chantal on the shoulder and then nodded. "You're a good person, Chantal," he said. "God is trying to bless you, so don't hinder it. His ways are not our ways, so don't try to understand everything. If you have been reading the Bible and praying, and if you believe that God has laid on your heart that He wants you to break up with Andy, then you have one thing left to do: be obedient."

Chantal sat in silence for a moment, processing Chris's words. "So, you really think God might get through to Andy?" she asked.

"I'll pray for that," Chris replied. "Don't stand in the way of that possibility. Just trust Him. Think of how blessed you are to hear from God so clearly."

CHAPTER 8

After school on Thursday, Lisa gazed at her cheerleading captain pleadingly. "Ally, I really want to practice my halftime routine once with JV before the game tonight," Lisa said. "Can I leave? The game starts in thirty-five minutes, and I still have to change into my uniform."

Ally Jordan bit her bottom lip. "Five more minutes? One more stunt? Can you give me that?" she asked.

Lisa sighed. "Okay," she surrendered. "I can give you that."

Five minutes quickly turned into twenty, and Lisa found herself running to the football field half in uniform and half in practice clothes. Panting, she reached the bleachers and pulled her skirt up over her warmup pants. She slid her warmup pants off and then pulled a pair of white leggings beneath her skirt. Quickly throwing her long hair up into a ponytail, she glanced over at the JV squad. She tied her shoes and brushed lint off of her skirt. Glancing at her watch, she widened her eyes. Kick-off was in seven minutes.

Lisa rushed over to Chantal and Leslie. "Can we run through halftime?" she gasped.

"Um, Lis, we just ran through it three times," Leslie said and shook her head. "No one has time to do it again. We have to line up in two minutes."

"What are you nervous about?" Chantal asked. "Is it a particular formation or dance sequence?"

"I just wanted to do it once with you guys in formation. I…I…I think I know where I'm supposed to stand…I think," Lisa stammered.

"None of the stunts have changed, or the interludes—just the dance. You're in the same spot as you've always been," Chantal assured her, "right up front."

Lisa sighed. "Will you switch spots with me?" she asked. "I don't want to be up front when I barely know the routine. Leslie and I practiced it for a couple of hours, but I'd like to have someone to follow."

"I'll switch with you," Chantal offered, "if you're that nervous about it."

Lisa nodded. "Thanks!" she exclaimed. "I owe you *big*, girl!"

⚜

Andy huddled with Jeff, Katherine, and Adam on the bleachers, trying to stay warm, while he waited for Chantal's halftime routine to begin. Chris, Bobby, and the JV team were playing well, considering the frigid temperature. Going into halftime, MLH was only ahead by one field goal. The fans were riled up and seemed anxious for the second half.

The girls' routine began with a loud cheer. Then the girls quickly mounted into a stunt. Lisa's stunt was up front and center when they sent her into a basket toss. With ease, she spread her legs into a Russian and landed safely in the arms of her bases and spotter.

"They're good," Andy said and Jeff.

"Lis hasn't practiced with them in weeks," Jeff stated, sounding concerned as he shook his head. "I always get scared that they're going to drop her."

After doing another cheer and chant, the girls got into their dance formation.

"That's weird. I didn't know Chantal was up front," Katherine said. "I thought Lisa was."

"Maybe she got sick of being up front for everything?" Jeff gathered.

When the music began blaring over the speakers, the girls lunged into a sixteen-count dance. Everything seemed to be flowing smoothly, until the V formation began to look more like an N.

"Does Lis have a solo part?" Katherine asked.

127

Andy squinted to better see what was happening on the field.

"I don't know," Jeff replied. "She looks confused."

"I don't think she knows the dance," Katherine stated. "I thought Leslie taught it to her on Monday?"

"Maybe she's confusing it with her varsity routine?" Adam suggested.

Andy watched in awe as Lisa stood still on the field and crossed her arms.

"The dance she was just doing is nothing like our varsity routine," Katherine said. "I've never seen that dance before in my life."

"I feel really bad for her," Jeff said, sounding angry. "I'll be back," he added, jumping up from his seat and running down the bleachers. When he reached the bottom, the girls were clearing the field.

CHAPTER 9

Lisa felt mortified as she ran off the field toward her boyfriend. The evident concern on his attractive face brought immediate comfort to her.

"What happened, hun?" Jeff asked as he placed his hand on her shoulder.

Lisa closed her eyes and shook her head. "What did I ever do to Leslie?" she blurted out as she shot her eyes open.

"Huh?" Jeff asked.

"She set me up!" Lisa exclaimed. "That dance I did was beat-for-beat what Leslie taught me on Monday."

Jeff glanced over at Leslie, who was engulfed in conversation with the other cheerleaders. "Why would she do that to you?" he asked. "You're her best friend."

Lisa shrugged. "That was so embarrassing. If any of the varsity girls saw that, they'll never ask me to be on their winter squad."

"Do you think Leslie's jealous that you practice with varsity?" Jeff asked quietly and nodded toward Leslie.

"Don't say that," Lisa hushed. "No one should be jealous of me."

Jeff shook his head. "Lisa, a lot of people are jealous of you. That's why you shouldn't trust *any* of these girls."

Lisa looked down at the ground and sighed. "Did I look that bad out there?" she asked hesitantly and slowly lifted her eyes to meet Jeff's baby blues.

"You looked beautiful," he replied and ran his fingertips over her flushed face.

⚜

"Thanks for coming to my game," Chantal said as she walked with Andy toward her mother's car. "I'm sorry that the halftime routine got messed up. Usually, it's a lot better. I hope you realize that was not Lisa's fault."

"Jeff explained to us what happened," Andy replied. "Do you think it was a misunderstanding between Lis and Lee?"

Chantal let out a heavy breath. "Maybe," she said.

"I'm glad that you invited me over for dinner tonight," Andy stated and took ahold of Chantal's hand. "I was hoping that we could talk for a bit afterwards."

"About what?" Chantal asked as her heart began pounding against her chest.

Andy shrugged. "It can wait until after dinner," he replied and squeezed her hand.

⚜

"Lisa! Lisa!" a loud voice called out, grabbing Lisa's attention as she was walking across the parking lot. She turned around and saw Ally running toward her.

Lisa's stomach dropped. It was bad enough that she had been humiliated in front of her boyfriend and friends by her "best friend." Now, her biggest fear seemed to be coming true. If Ally was still at school, then she had most likely stayed for the football game. As Ally caught up to her, Lisa could feel her face grow red.

"Lisa, you must want to kill me! I am *so* sorry," Ally said earnestly as she shook her head apologetically. "I asked you for five minutes, took twenty, and caused a mess. I am *so* sorry that you did not get to practice with JV. That was selfish of me. I can't imagine how hard it must be for you to be part of JV *and* varsity. I saw what happened at halftime, and it put me in my place. I'm working you way too hard for an alternate position, and you're putting in way too much effort. I just got off the phone with Denise, and we both think you've earned a full-time spot on varsity."

"What?!" Lisa cried, widening her eyes and dropping her jaw to the pavement.

130

Ally nodded. "For the rest of the playoff games and for basketball in the winter, we'd like you on the squad."

Lisa smiled widely and threw her arms around Ally. "Thank you! Thank you so much!" she exclaimed.

Later that night, Lisa called Jeff and shared the good news about varsity cheer. "You're kidding," he said while holding his cell phone to his ear.

"No, seriously! Ally put me on her squad!" Lisa's voice rang through the phone. "I can't believe how it worked out. I never would have thought she'd see it that way! I thought for sure I blew my chances of ever making the winter squad. I never thought in a million years that I'd be pulled onto varsity for the rest of the football games. Jeff! That could even be for the Superbowl!"

"That's awesome, Lis," Jeff said enthusiastically, finding it hard not to laugh at the irony of the situation. "I am so happy for you. I bet you can't wait to rub it in Leslie's face, huh?"

"I'm so happy right now that I don't think I could be mean to anyone," Lisa replied. "If she hadn't totally screwed me over, then I never would have been asked onto the squad. I don't even want to find out her motive right now. It would probably kill my mood."

"I'm not going away with her," Jeff stated matter-of-factly. "What she did was psychotic."

"Yeah, I'm going to have to talk to her," Lisa said. "I don't want this to ruin Andy's trip though. He's been through so much lately, you know?"

"This would be a complete different conversation if Ally hadn't put you on varsity," Jeff commented uneasily. "Leslie could have easily ruined your chance of making the winter squad. Don't let her off so easily."

"That's true," Lisa agreed. "I'm so glad her plan backfired," she laughed. "It's humorous."

"Do you want me to talk to her?" Jeff asked, grimacing as he pictured Leslie's fake smile.

Lisa laughed. "No. I think I can handle her on my own, buddy," she replied. "But thanks for the offer."

"All right. Well, then let me know her excuse after you talk to her," Jeff said. "As of right now, I'm done being friends with her. I love you, Lisa, and I want anyone who crosses you out of our lives."

"I'll let you know what she says," Lisa agreed, sounding like she cared a lot less about Leslie's betrayal than Jeff did. "Goodnight, lover."

"Sweet dreams, beautiful," Jeff replied. Lisa's cheerful tone made him happy, but he feared that the good fortune of the event would masque Leslie's cruelty.

⁂

Katherine sighed as her phone began vibrating on her desk. A picture of her and Bobby appeared on the screen. "Here goes nothing," she said as she picked up her phone. "Hello?" she called into it, hearing the nervousness in her tone.

"Is it the right time to talk yet?" Bobby asked.

Katherine sighed. "You played a really good game tonight. Are you sure you want to kill the buzz of that with a serious convo?" she asked.

"It's hard for me to enjoy anything when I know something isn't right with you," Bobby replied.

Katherine fell silent. *He sounds like he cares so much,* she thought. *Why doesn't that matter to me?*

"You didn't cheat on me, did you?" Bobby questioned her.

"What?!" Katherine exclaimed, completely caught off guard by his words. "I would never cheat on you!"

"Then why are you acting so distant?" Bobby asked. "You're even distant from your best friends."

"Woah! Why would I be distant from my friends if I cheated on you?" Katherine questioned him.

"I don't know."

"That's crazy. I cannot believe you think I would cheat on you!"

"I don't think you did! I just wanted to make sure. You are acting so weird, lately. I know something must be going on—something bigger than PMS."

Katherine widened her eyes with anger. "Rude! That was wicked rude!" she yelled into her phone.

"Rude is you not telling me what is going on, Kat!" Bobby retorted.

"Fine! Why am I distant from my friends? I'm not like them, and I can't trust them! I don't want to be close with people I can't trust. The way they backstab each other is pathetic. I'm fed up with the gossip, the rumors, the snobby attitudes, and the popularity contests,"

Katherine vented. "I don't fit in with them anymore. Day after day, I just sit there quietly and pretend to listen."

"What?! That is crazy! Kat, you fit in with them. Everyone associates you with them. What are you talking about?" Bobby questioned her.

"Exactly! That is my point! I don't want to be associated with them," Katherine stated seriously. "Ever since I started hanging out with Chantal, I've been happier. Her friends are nice. I actually trust them not to twist my words into a rumor. Lee, Lis, Cathy, and Julianna are too obsessed with their social lives to care about each other. I'm not like that Bobby. I don't even like to drink. Lisa and Leslie tricked me into eating pot brownies when I was thirteen! I should have stopped hanging out with them back then. They had no respect for my morals."

"At Jeff's party? They were drunk. Lisa doesn't even drink anymore," Bobby said.

"It's the principle of the thing!" Katherine exclaimed. "I can't hang out with people like that anymore. I want friends I can trust."

"Oh, like Jon Anderson?" Bobby taunted. "Jon's not the angel you think he is. I know so much dirt about that kid. He has hooked up with so many girls; he probably has an STD."

At the sound of Bobby's words, Katherine was barely able to stop herself from throwing her phone across her room. "Listen to yourself!" she screamed. "Everything you say is negative. You, Jeff, and Andy do that *all the time*. You glorify each other and make it sound like anyone who isn't in our 'clique' sucks."

"Actually, I think we're pretty nice to people," Bobby stated defensively.

"To their faces!" Katherine cried in disgust.

"So, you'd rather us be mean to their faces?" Bobby asked. "What do you want me to do? Be friends with *everyone*?"

"No, but you don't have to put people down all the time," Katherine replied immediately. "I really like the senior girls I cheer with because they're humble and real. I'm learning a lot from them, and I think they might even be rubbing off on Lisa. I want our grade to be like theirs. They're not cliquey. No one tries to act like they're better than anyone. They realize people have different talents and different strengths, so they don't judge each other. Ally Jordan and Michelle Taylor make everyone feel welcome.

"The way our grade behaves is *horrific*. When I realized that I was part of the snobbiest clique of all, I had to take a step back," Katherine admitted, knowing that her words would surely anger Bobby. "And that's where I'm at right now."

"Oh, so, you think we're snobs?"

"When was the last time you said hi to someone you don't hang out with on a regular basis?"

"So, you're saying that I'm not friendly enough to be your boyfriend?"

"I didn't say that. I'm just explaining myself…like you asked me to," Katherine stated defensively.

"Well, what's the point of having a boyfriend you don't want to hang out with?"

Katherine sighed. "I told you the other day. You can either stick by me while I figure things out or let me go."

"Well, what do you want more? Do you even know?" Bobby asked, sounding more irritated than hurt. "It really sucks that this is happening right before Christmas!"

"Why don't we just see how things go over vacation?" Katherine suggested.

"Oh, so, you're still going to come away with us snobs?" Bobby retorted. "Oh, wait. That makes sense—Anderson is coming!"

"That's enough! I'm going to bed," Katherine stated angrily. "Good night. I'll see you tomorrow in homeroom."

"Right, because you can't meet a snob like me at my locker," Bobby muttered.

"Good night," Katherine said and hung up her phone abruptly.

Chapter 10

After dinner, Andy and Chantal sat on her bedroom couch and stared anxiously at each other. For what felt like hours, neither of them spoke a word. Chantal grabbed ahold of Andy's hand and gazed at him affectionately.

"I love you so much, Chantal," Andy said and put his head down.

"I love you, too," Chantal said and squeezed his hand.

"I want to tell you what happened to me when I was in a coma," Andy said and glanced up at her hesitantly. His heart was racing. He couldn't stand the feeling of holding the story in or the thought of letting it out. "I haven't told anyone."

"What do you mean?" Chantal asked. "The dream you had?"

Andy bit his bottom lip. "I don't think it was just a dream," he replied.

"What do you mean it wasn't a dream?" Chantal asked.

"I'm going to tell you a story—a *long* story—about a group of kids that went away for a recovery celebration," Andy said. "I don't want to freak you out, especially since we are going away soon for my recovery celebration. But if you will let me, I'd like to explain what happened, from beginning to end."

"Sure," Chantal agreed, displaying more concern than curiosity in her facial expression and tone.

Andy told Chantal everything that had happened at Fallen Lake. He told her first how he had experienced it, and then he told her the entire story. Chantal listened quietly. At times, it had been clear to Andy that she was fighting back a reaction, but she had remained completely silent. Andy could tell that her analytical mind had already begun piecing the puzzle together. He assumed that what had taken him three weeks to figure out would only take Chantal a few minutes. Sure enough, after a moment of complete silence, Chantal's green eyes grew wide. Andy raised his eyebrows at her expectantly.

She nodded slowly. "I think you're right," she said. "I don't think it was just a dream."

"So, now, do you get what I meant when I said I had to figure out where my feet were planted?" Andy asked.

"Yeah," Chantal said and put her head down.

"What's wrong?" Andy asked and nudged her playfully.

Chantal sighed and looked up at him. She looked like she was on the verge of tears. "I'm just overwhelmed by what you just told me and by what it could mean. There's a lot that's been going on with me that you don't know about, and it kind of coincides with your story. I think I just need a night to process it all and pray about everything."

Andy nodded. "Okay, that's understandable. You're not mad at me, are you?"

"No," Chantal said firmly.

"Good, because I was worried about the Leslie thing," Andy admitted.

Chantal showed no reaction to his confession. She appeared lost in thought. "Why don't we hang out again tomorrow night?" she suggested after a moment. "We can talk about everything then."

"Sounds good," Andy agreed, feeling like a thousand bricks had been lifted off of his shoulders.

Chapter 11

Leslie's voice echoed through the freshman locker hall on Friday morning, "Lisa! Wait up! Talk to me!" Lisa, hearing Leslie loud and clear, paused for a split second and then continued walking down the hall with Jeff.

Seconds later, Leslie caught up to them and latched herself onto Lisa's arm. "I need to talk to you about yesterday," she said, breathing heavily.

"Honestly, Leslie, we don't want you to talk to us," Jeff said and pushed Leslie's hand off of Lisa's arm.

Leslie gazed at Lisa pleadingly. "Lis, my own boyfriend won't even speak to me," she said. "Can we please straighten this out?"

Lisa threw her arms up in the air. "I don't really know what there is to straighten out," she said. "Either you taught me the wrong dance by mistake, or you really wanted me to look like an idiot. Pick one."

"It wasn't my fault," Leslie whined. "When the captains found out that I taught you the dance they changed part of it. They're really annoyed that you don't practice with us anymore. They told me not to teach you anything else. I felt terrible all week, but I didn't know what to do."

"I don't get it, Lee," Jeff stated while shaking his head. "You call Lisa your best friend but throw her under the bus for your captains?"

"Did all the girls know about this?" Lisa asked, hoping that the pain of that thought did not ring through in her tone. The look in Jeff's eyes told her that it did.

Leslie shook her head. "No," she said, "none of them did. Jackie and Laura pulled me aside at practice on Tuesday."

"Lisa, listen to me," Jeff said, placing his hands on her shoulders and leaning into her. "A true friend does not do what Leslie did," he said and shook his head.

Lisa gazed sorrowfully into Jeff's compassionate blue eyes.

"You don't need anyone in your life who puts other people on the line for her own selfish motives," Jeff stated loudly and firmly. "You have two brothers, me, Andy, Katherine, Cathy, Adam, and Bobby. We all love you, and we have your back. Crap like that does not belong in your life."

Lisa swallowed the large lump in her throat and nodded. She turned to where Leslie had been standing to see that she was completely out of sight.

Cathy was placing her backpack in her locker when she heard a nearby group of girls begin gawking. She glanced at the girls strangely and then turned to see what the big deal was. As her green eyes peered down the locker hall, a smile spread across her face. Every girl in the hall had their eyes glued on the same sight: Marc Dunkin and Luke Davids. They were strolling through the sea of freshmen, smiling with amusement, and heading toward Cathy's locker.

"What are you guys doing in the freshman locker hall?!" Cathy exclaimed loudly.

"Good morning, Miss Cathy," Luke greeted her with a high five. "You feel like going out for breakfast?"

"Breakfast? Now?" Cathy asked and raised her eyebrows at Marc.

Marc laughed. "What better time for breakfast than during first period?"

"I've heard about your breakfast adventures," Cathy said playfully. She crossed her arms as she attempted to quell the butterflies in her stomach.

Luke and Marc looked at each other and laughed.

"Only good things, I'm sure," Luke said and patted Cathy on the shoulder.

"Ri-iii-ght," she said gradually. "Well, I can't skip class today. I'm trying to get my parents' permission for New Year's, so I can't risk getting in trouble."

"Why? What's going on for New Year's?" Luke asked.

Cathy lowered her eyebrows and glanced from Luke to Marc. "I thought you guys were thinking of going to Loon," she replied matter-of-factly.

"Oh, yeah," Luke said, "either Loon or a party at my house. I didn't know you were coming. That's chill though."

Cathy found it odd that Marc hadn't told Luke he'd invited her. She wondered if Luke was just playing dumb.

"Any luck with that whole permission thing?" Marc asked.

"I got a conditional yes," Cathy said hesitantly, "after a lot of questions I couldn't answer."

"Well, I was wrong. My friends didn't rent a condo," Marc said. "It's Michelle's parents' place. It looks like a bust because they're going to be there."

"Oh, really?" Cathy asked in surprise. "Then I'd probably be able to go! My parents are friends with her parents."

Marc glanced at Luke and then shrugged. "We'll see," he said. "It also depends on how many people they let her invite."

"Oh, I didn't know it was limited," Cathy said.

Marc shrugged. "Michelle loves me. I can talk her into anything," he said and smiled at Cathy, which made her feel weak at the knees.

"Alright, let's head out," Luke said and patted Marc on the back while nodding toward the exit. "Take it easy, CK."

"Bye!" Cathy sang playfully, thoroughly enjoying their attention.

"I'll call you later or something," Marc called loudly. He gazed back at Cathy as he followed Luke toward the door. "We can talk about New Year's."

Cathy smiled at him and then began heading to homeroom. After her tumultuous breakup with Jason, Cathy had feared losing all of her friends. Although Lisa, Leslie, and Julianna had remained loyal to her, most people had sided with Jason. However, right after their breakup, Marc had started messaging Cathy on a regular basis and inviting her out with him and Luke.

By hanging out with them, Cathy had a chance to observe the girls in their group. At first, she couldn't understand why they were so nice to each other. She couldn't fathom how party-girl Missy Kent could be friends with straightedge Day Angeletti. Or how Ally Jordan, Katie McKnight, and Laurelle Mahoney had all dated Matt Davids yet still remained friends. They were all so different in style and personality. Seeing how Cathy's friends had always turned into clones of each other, she was amazed by the diversity.

After a short time, Cathy realized that the way the senior girls treated each other worked. Despite their differences, they accepted each other. During the handful of times Cathy had hung out with them, there had been no drama. They seemed to genuinely adore, respect, and encourage one another. They had even been friendly to Cathy—a random freshman—the very first time Marc invited her out with him. They spoke highly of people who didn't hang out with them. It had shocked Cathy to see that the most popular girls at MLH didn't even care if people knew their names.

Chapter 12

Katherine glanced up and bit her bottom lip in thought as Bobby and Andy walked into their homeroom. Bobby and Andy took their seats and continued talking without glancing in Katherine's direction. Katherine lowered her eyebrows and crossed her arms. She had at least expected a hello from Andy. After all, he sat beside her!

After a few seconds, Katherine realized that the boys were just engulfed in their conversation and not intentionally ignoring her. "What are you guys talking about?" she asked and glanced curiously from Bobby to Andy.

"Lisa didn't tell you?" Bobby asked. "What happened at my game yesterday was Leslie's fault. Her captains made her teach Lisa the wrong dance. Jeff thinks that they're all jealous of her—everyone, including Leslie."

"Not everyone," Andy chimed in. "Not Chantal."

"Well, yeah," Bobby agreed. "Not Chantal."

Katherine squinted. "What?" she questioned them. "Why would everyone be jealous of Lisa and not Natalie? Natalie did the right dance."

"Who's Natalie?" Andy and Bobby asked in unison.

"The other girl from JV who practices with us," Katherine replied. "Ally is going to flip out when she hears about what happened.

The JV captains would have to be pretty stupid to not see that coming. I know it's the end of the season, but Ally would probably suspend them for next season for this. They know how rigid she is."

Andy stared blankly at Katherine for a moment, looking as if he were in deep thought. "Something's not adding up right," he stated flatly.

⁘

Leslie ran into her first-period history class, hoping to beat Lisa there. Andy, Alyssa, Bryan, Jon, and Chantal were already in their seats. She glanced at them warily, wondering if they had all heard about the football game.

"Hi, Lee!" Alyssa greeted her. "Sit next to me! I want to talk about your lake house."

Leslie let out a deep breath and quickly took a seat beside Alyssa. She had never appreciated Alyssa's friendliness more. Andy and Chantal had both looked at Leslie strangely when she took her seat. Bryan had nodded and smiled at her, staying as neutral as always. Jon seemed completely oblivious to her presence; he was reading what appeared to be a very interesting book—definitely not their history curriculum.

"So, are we going to be away for New Year's?" Alyssa asked. "My brother invited me to go skiing, but I wasn't sure if I'd be away."

"I think that's the plan," Leslie said and glanced uneasily at Andy. "They usually have a New Year's party at the community center every year. It's not bad."

"Maybe I could meet up with my brother and ski one of the days," Alyssa said thoughtfully. "How far away are you from Loon?"

"Maybe twenty-five minutes at the most," Leslie replied. "Maybe we could all go skiing for a day. Andy mentioned something about wanting to ski."

A moment later, Lisa walked into the classroom and took a seat in front of Andy. She opened her binder and began looking over her notes without glancing in Leslie's direction. Nothing about Lisa seemed tense or stressed.

"So, Bobby told me that they pulled you up to varsity, full time," Andy said loudly as he tapped on Lisa's back. "You must be excited."

Lisa turned around and smiled. "Yeah, I was shocked. I thought my chances of making the winter squad were ruined."

"God must want you on that squad," Chantal stated. "Stuff like that doesn't just happen!"

Lisa nodded. "It's interesting how it worked out. I could not have planned it that way."

"Well, someone did," Andy remarked sarcastically. "I just doubt they received their expected outcome."

"I'm happy with the way everything worked out," Lisa said and glanced at Leslie.

Leslie felt every muscle in her body go tense.

"I don't think Jeff is," Andy commented dryly. "He told us that if we go to Leslie's cottage, then we are no longer his friends."

Okay, are they seriously talking about me as if I am not even here? Leslie wondered. *Don't they know I can hear them?*

Lisa rolled her eyes. "He'll cool off. I love my over-protective boyfriend, even when he's this ridiculous. If I'm still up for the trip, he has no reason not to be."

Andy dropped his jaw. "You're still going?" he asked.

"As long as you are," Lisa replied. "The trip isn't about me; it's about your recovery."

Andy raised his eyebrows. "You know, you're pretty amazing sometimes," he said appreciatively.

"I do what I can," Lisa said and winked at Chantal.

Chantal leaned toward Lisa and whispered something to her. Leslie was unable to decipher Chantal's words. If there was anyone she hated seeing Lisa grow closer with, it was Chantal. A few seconds later, Lisa leaned back and smiled. "Thanks," she said.

CHAPTER 13

Before second period, Andy walked up to Leslie in the corridor and eyed her expectantly. He crossed his arms and peered at her, assuming that she would catch his drift.

She glanced at him warily. For once, she appeared flustered.

Andy gazed at her sternly. "We have five minutes before the bell rings. Can you explain why I've been pinned between a rock and a hard place?" he asked.

Leslie looked distressed as she peered at him. "Andy, I never meant for *any* of this to happen," she began. "I heard what you said to Lisa in history, and I'm sorry if Jeff's putting pressure on you. I can cancel the trip if you want."

"Lee, did you really teach Lisa the wrong dance?" Andy asked, shaking his head in disapproval.

Leslie sighed. "Ally told Jackie and Laura, my captains, that she was considering Lisa for a full-time varsity spot. She said that being in between two squads seemed to be stressing Lisa out. When they found out that I taught Lisa the new dance, they told me what Ally said. They were both annoyed with the situation and wanted her to just cheer full time with varsity. They knew Ally was going to be at the game, so they changed the dance and told me not tell Lisa. They assured me that it would get her pulled up to varsity. I knew that was what Lisa wanted.

I did it for that reason, but Jeff won't give me a chance to explain that to her."

Andy stared blankly at Leslie. "So, you taught Lisa the wrong dance so she could get promoted?" Andy questioned her. He shook his head and eyed her skeptically.

"When I taught her the dance, it was the right one. They did not change it until afterwards," Leslie replied. "I didn't tell her about the change so that she could get promoted. Lisa never would have messed up intentionally, even to secure herself a varsity spot."

"Well, what about the other girl who practices with varsity?" Andy asked. "Are the captains annoyed with her situation, too?"

Leslie seemed caught off guard by Andy's words. "Um, I don't know," Leslie stammered. "I don't know Natalie or anything about her situation."

"You definitely need to talk to Lisa," Andy stated. "I kind of get why you wanted to help her out, but I don't agree with what you did. You don't really know your captains. What if they had lied and Ally was not really considering Lisa for her squad? What if they were just jealous of Lisa and wanted to humiliate her? They could have just been trying to cause division between the two of you. You never know what people's motives are. You and Lisa are both lucky that was not the case. She's happy with the outcome, but I don't blame her for feeling deceived."

"So, you think I'm a horrible person?" Leslie implied and glanced at Andy shamefully.

"No, I don't think you're a horrible person," Andy said and placed his hand on Leslie's shoulder. "I just think you owe her an apology."

Leslie nodded. "You're right; it could have turned out so much worse," she agreed and stared blankly ahead.

"All right, Lee. I have to run to class," Andy said and patted her shoulder. "I'll tell Lisa to talk to you, if I see her."

Leslie smiled widely. "Thank you!" she cried.

❦

"No way, dude!" Jeff exclaimed, eyeing Andy in disbelief during their biology lab. "I am *not* going away with that girl. You can believe her lies if you want. Legit, I'm chill."

"You think she's lying?" Andy questioned him.

"Are you kidding me? Of course, she's lying! Once she heard that Lisa got asked onto varsity her mind went into overdrive making up that story. She said nothing to Lisa this morning about it being for her own good. She tried to pin all the blame on her captains," Jeff replied. "Leslie is smart, manipulative, and charming. She's pretty much the girl version of you."

Chantal, who was sitting beside Andy, let out a short laugh.

Andy rolled his eyes at Jeff. "Thanks a lot, dude," he said dryly.

"I'm kidding. But seriously, I saw her true colors a long time ago," Jeff stated. "Don't be so naïve, Rosetti. If Adam's all set with her, then you should know this was the straw that broke the camel's back. There's way more to the situation than either one of us will ever know."

Andy stared at Jeff, wondering what he was implying.

Chapter 14

Katherine and Bobby entered the cafeteria in deep discussion. "Can't you see what I mean?" Katherine asked. "I picked up on Leslie's character a long time ago. Trust me, there's a reason why I'm breaking away from her."

"It's pretty crappy what she did to Lisa," Bobby stated flatly, "but I don't see what your issue is with the rest of us. Lisa has always been a good friend to you, and I think I've treated you all right."

"You have," Katherine agreed, "and Lisa has been a good friend."

"So, you just like Chantal's friends better than us?" Bobby asked.

Katherine bit her bottom lip and crossed her arms as she took her place in the lunch line. "You know, I don't know what it is, but they just make me happy."

"Chantal and Chris are two of the happiest people I know," Bobby said, "so I see where you're coming from. Our friends really aren't that positive all the time."

"Sometimes, I just feel trapped in a world I know I don't belong in and can't get out of," Katherine said slowly. "There's a lot I want to explain to you. I'm so much better at writing out my thoughts than verbalizing them. I hope you don't think it's weird, but I wrote you a letter."

Bobby laughed. "You what? A letter? That's kind of cute, Kat," he said.

Katherine pulled the letter out of her binder. "You might want to wait until you sit down to read it," she said as she handed it to him. "I don't think 'cute' is really the best word for it," she added.

Bobby's smile faded. He took the folded paper and put it in his pocket. "Can't wait to read it," he said dryly.

Bobby,

I want to be open and honest with you. You know how shy I am and that I always hold part of myself back. I think you deserve the full truth of what I have been feeling. I'm sorry if you think a letter is less personal than face-to-face conversation. It is just the only way I could get my thoughts in order. So, here goes...

I feel trapped in a world that I do not belong in, almost like I'm bound by rope and need someone to break the bonds. So many people have come and tried to break them for me, but they can't. I just sit there bound to my insecurities, fears, and anxieties, feeling helpless. The world seems so dark, the one I'm bound in. It's filled with false promises of freedom that just make me realize how empty I am. It's like every time another person comes along to untie me, my hopes rise that maybe he or she will be the one to set me free. When reality sets in, I realize it was just a false hope, just like the last person who could not break my bonds.

Then unexpectedly light begins to flood the darkness, and I see people running around freely. They're not bound by rope or stuck in the darkness; they're free. So, I watch them for a little while because something about them is captivating. Then I realize that they have something I want. So, I stare at them in amazement, wishing I could ask them how they broke free. They can't hear me because they're too far away. I let out a cry for help, even though I think it might be hopeless. Then the light begins to spread, and it comes closer to me. The people are right in front of me now, and if I were not bound, I could reach out and touch them. To my surprise, as the light draws closer, the bonds begin to tighten. I'm sure the rope would choke me just to keep me in its realm.

Then someone in the light looks at me with kind eyes, and I just know that he is the answer to my cry for help—the cry so drowned out that no one could have heard it with ears. I stop struggling and just stare at him in awe. He begins speaking to me, words that, at first, I cannot understand. So, I begin to listen more carefully, and I start to believe in what he is saying. I realize the more I believe the looser the rope feels. Then I think, how is that possible? The rope was just suffocating me, and no one could loosen it. How can I be getting closer to freedom just by believing?

Then the person tells me, the bonds can be set free, but they'll grab me again and tie me up even tighter if I do not have a refuge. I think how can I get one? Then my heart breaks as he tells me.

All the bad things that I have done that bound me to the dark world left me worthy of nothing besides eternal bondage. Then I hear about someone I've never known, who loved me enough to pay the price to set me free forever. I think, what do I have to do for this person? How can I make it up to him? How could he love me so much? Then the person in the light tells me all I have to do is believe. I almost laugh because I've tried everything in my power to break free. I think, are you kidding me? I just have to believe?

So, I take a leap of faith and let it sink into my heart. Immediately, I am encamped by light and feel freer than I ever imagined possible. I know at that very moment, I'll never be able to look at life the same way. I've entered into a whole new world; I've been delivered from the darkness. And it is there I find happiness.

That is where I am at and what I have experienced. I know this is all metaphorical, but I hope you can read between the lines and understand what I am trying to say. Take all the time you need and ask me whatever you'd like. — Love, Kat

Katherine stared at Bobby while he read her letter. She tried to recall what she had written. She was nervous for Bobby's reaction. He was far from a poet. He wasn't a "read between the lines" kind of person. He probably had wanted a more direct explanation, but when she had written it, her main concern was putting her own thoughts in order. She had barely considered Bobby's reaction.

Bobby put the letter down. "That's a really messed up metaphor, Kat," he said flatly and glanced at her strangely. "I wonder if Andy felt like that when he was trapped in a coma."

"Surrounded by darkness?" Katherine asked. "Hmm. I never thought to ask him what being in a coma was like."

"Me either," Bobby said and shook his head. "I hope it wasn't anything like you described."

"Most people probably don't even realize they are in darkness," Katherine said, "but that doesn't take away from its existence. Jon, Chantal, Chris, and their friends are the people in the light in my letter."

"So, go dance in the light," Bobby retorted. "What do you want from me? Permission? I can't give you that. I don't have what they have. I don't understand them. I don't want to understand them. I just want to know if I'm supposed to return your Christmas present. I want to know if you're going to be my girlfriend tomorrow. Are we going to spend New Year's at Leslie's? I want to know what is going on with us, in this life, right here, right now—not what's going on in some metaphorical spiritual realm!"

Katherine stared at Bobby blankly, appearing unmoved by his sudden emotional outburst. She did not care about her Christmas present or her New Year's plans. At that moment, she did not even care about being Bobby's girlfriend. It suddenly seemed only trivial, as did many of the things that used to worry her.

In October, Katherine had not wanted to attend Alyssa's Halloween party; she had just been dumped and wanted nothing to do with people like Alyssa, Jason, or Chris. She would never have even gone if Leslie had not talked her into it. That was the night she found out about Andy's accident, the first night she had felt distant from Bobby, and the night Jon Anderson had entered her life.

Looking back, Katherine could see God's fingerprints all over that situation. The phone cutting out at the exact moment Bobby said, "I don't think I want to go out (pause) anymore." *A dropped call in the middle of a supposed breakup? What were the odds of that?* It reminded her of a cell phone commercial.

She never would have gone to Alyssa's party if she had not been so upset over Bobby. Never had she expected to see Jon Anderson at the party; he had just broken up with the host! Katherine remembered seeing Jon across Alyssa's kitchen and becoming overwhelmed with curiosity. She had tried to imagine what could have brought him there.

Jon had always been "cute" in her opinion, but nothing about him had ever stood out to her. After talking to him at Alyssa's party, she had walked away wondering what he was about. Although she had been preoccupied with thoughts of Bobby, Jon had managed to catch her attention.

That same night, something else significant had occurred. Chris Dunkin had been nice to her, nicer than anyone else at the party. He had acted nothing like the rebellious kid she remembered from middle school, and what he did for her that night left an impression on her. She had realized that something significant had taken hold of Chris's life.

That night, she had also found out about Andy's accident. It had seemed so tragic at the time, but looking back, Katherine realized it was a blessing in many ways. Watching everyone come together for Andy's prayer service had made Katherine see how powerless people were on their own.

From the sidelines, Katherine had studied Chantal's, Jon's, and Chris's reactions to Andy's tragedy. She had compared them to her own friends' attitudes. The strength Chantal, Jon, and Chris had exhibited was beyond Katherine's understanding.

Jon had begun conversing with her frequently, and she had found herself growing more and more intrigued. Eventually, it got to the point that Katherine wanted to spend time with Jon more than anyone else. He listened to her with compassion and offered her advice deeper than "drink it off" or "get laid." He had more wisdom than the average teenager. In a way, Jon became a guide for Katherine.

When Jon first began sharing his faith with Katherine, a red flag had waved before her eyes. She did not know why, but all she had wanted to do was run from him every time he mentioned Jesus. The desire to run made no sense to her because she respected Jon for his Christian values.

Just when she thought she had all she could handle of Jon's Christian banter, Jason and Jessie had entered her life. If Lisa, Leslie, and Cathy had not treated Jessie callously, Katherine never would have pushed past her anxieties and talked to Jessie. Katherine had expected Jessie to be sweet, but Jason's kindness had completely surprised her. She discovered that she actually enjoyed his company. She had the privilege of watching him transform from an edgy punk into a considerate person. He, like Chris, said God had changed his life.

Looking at Jason, reflecting on Jon's words, remembering what Chris had been like in middle school, and comparing the light in their lives to the darkness in her friends' lives, Katherine decided that she wanted to find a more positive path to travel along. Jon had been a significant source of light in her life, helping her find that path.

At Andy's dinner party, when Mr. and Mrs. Rosetti had spoken of Chantal's devotion to God, Katherine had made the decision that she wanted to know what being spiritual really meant. Katherine's parents were very religious, but they were not spiritual. She realized that Jon could talk to her about Christ non-stop until the day he died, but she still wouldn't know Him. "Knowing about God" and "knowing God" were two completely different things—something Katherine had not realized until she became acquainted with Jon.

After Andy's dinner party, Katherine had called Jon. As usual, he had been happy to hear from her. Once she mentioned her interest in developing a relationship with God, Jon had become ecstatic. He did not even question what probably seemed like a sudden decision on her part, and she respected his tact.

Looking back at Alyssa's party, Katherine could see how God had worked to get her attention. She could see how He had orchestrated circumstances in her life to reveal Himself to her. There had been too many "coincidences" for her to believe any longer in coincidence. She could go all day long playing the "what if" game—if Cathy had not invited Julianna to Alyssa's party… if her phone had not cut out at that exact moment… if Andy had not gone outside after Lady… if Chris had not offered to help her look for her friends… if Jason hadn't fought Sean O'Leary… if Lisa had not made up rumors about Jessie in an attempt to support Cathy… if Jason had not been in so many of her classes… if Bobby hadn't grown so distant because of Andy's coma… if JV football games hadn't tied up Bobby, Lisa, and Leslie. Her circumstantial "what if" list could have gone on and on.

Jon had explained to Katherine that no one desires a relationship with God through faith in Christ without having first been handpicked by God. He said that God reveals Himself to anyone who asks in faith, believing that Jesus Christ paid his or her sins' penalty of death on the Cross. In Katherine's metaphor, Jon had been the one in the light, and Jesus had been her refuge. Her metaphor had become her reality.

Chapter 15

Squished between Jeff and Cathy at her lunch table, Lisa felt the hairs on her arms rise. She glanced up and saw Leslie taking a seat next to Andy. Jeff nudged Lisa in the side and nodded in Leslie's direction. "Don't say anything," Lisa whispered to her boyfriend.

Adam, who was sitting on the other side of Andy, rose from the table and walked away without uttering a word. Leslie put her head down and stared blankly at her lunch. Jeff turned to Lisa. "Let's go sit with Jay," he said loudly.

Lisa sighed. "I want to eat with Cathy," she replied.

"Why do you want to sit with Jason?" Cathy asked, leaning over Lisa and eyeing Jeff strangely.

"Because of Leslie, obviously," Jeff replied loudly.

Cathy glanced at Leslie and then back at Jeff. "What's wrong with Lee?" she asked.

"Have you not told *anyone* about what she did to you?" Jeff asked Lisa.

Lisa shook her head. "Jeff, please don't make a big deal out of this. I don't want anyone talking about my life." She glanced at him pleadingly, hoping that he would see how serious she was. He blinked and nodded slightly. Then he put his arm around her and pulled her closer to him.

"So, Leslie," Bobby stated loudly from the other side of Jeff. "Why don't you tell us what happened at my game yesterday? I heard that there was a lot of confusion during halftime while we were in the locker room."

Leslie looked up at Bobby and took a deep breath.

"Dude, come on. Now's not the time," Andy said and shook his head at Bobby.

"Why not? It's on all of our minds. We kind of need to know if we're going away with her," Bobby replied unapologetically. "So, what's the deal, Lee?"

Leslie's face turned bright red.

Well, that's just great, Bobby, Lisa thought. *You are in a bad mood, so now everyone has to feel awkward and miserable?* "It was just a misunderstanding!" Lisa exclaimed and widened her eyes. "Can we *not* talk about this? Please?"

Cathy squinted her eyes in obvious confusion and glanced from Lisa to Leslie. "Lee, do you want to come with me to the bathroom?" she asked.

Leslie glanced at Cathy and immediately stood up from the table. Without waiting for Cathy to rise, Leslie stormed off toward the cafeteria's bathroom.

"What happened?" Cathy asked Lisa. Without waiting for a response, she rushed after Leslie.

Lisa rested her forehead in her hands and sighed. She felt Jeff's hand on her back. "That just confirmed her guilt to me," he stated. "Lis, I can't believe you're going to let her get away with deceiving you."

"Can't you see it now? What I was saying about Leslie?" Katherine asked, turning toward Bobby and placing her hand on his arm. Bobby rolled his eyes and sighed. Katherine turned toward Lisa. "Lis, someone once told me that if a wise person contends with a fool, whether the fool rages or laughs, there will be no peace," she said.

Lisa paused for a moment to let Katherine's words sink in. *In other words,* she thought, *Leslie is not worth my time.* "Thanks," Lisa said quietly.

Andy glanced from Lisa to Chantal. "I know now for certain that Fallen Lake was not just a dream," he said quietly to her. Lisa stared at him curiously, wondering what dream he was referring to.

"Yeah," Chantal agreed.

Lisa glanced from Chantal to Andy. "What dream?" she asked.

"I'll tell you later," Andy said. By the look in his green eyes, Lisa could tell that Andy had a lot to say.

CHAPTER 16

<u>Andy Rosetti</u>

So, let's talk. Let's do the last thing any normal person would want to do: an overly analytical self-evaluation. Take a look at what you know about me, just from what my friends and I have shared with you. I was sort of the guy who had it all, you know? I had a respectable girlfriend, good grades, a great reputation, popular friends, a good relationship with my parents and teachers, many admirers, and a highly respected student council position. I had a resumé full of charitable activities and community service that I had participated in. On paper, I looked like someone who had it all together. Actually, even off paper, I looked like I did. Oh, believe me, I was a pro at flashing that good-old fake smile.

It seems like just when you think you have everything figured out, life throws you a curve ball. A tornado in Montgomery? Now, who would ever expect that? Certainly not a self-confident fifteen-year-old-freshman at MLH. Dorothy woke up in Oz, where there was good and evil. Dorothy lucked out. When I woke up in Fallen Lake, I woke up to my life.

Do you worry more about your outward appearance than your heart's attitude? Would you rather remain oblivious to the truth about yourself than face what you really are? For fifteen years, I lived naïve to the truth. If anyone had asked me that question, I would have answered, "I know who I am." I'm sure my voice would have been filled with attitude. Isn't life just a bit more comfortable when it's not being examined under a bright light—when small flaws can go unnoticed and true colors are left unexposed?

So, I woke up in Fallen Lake; you know the story. What a nightmare, right? How comfortably can you sit on the following statement? **What appeared to happen to me in Fallen Lake actually happened to me in Montgomery.** Ponder on that.

I said I woke up to my life in Fallen Lake. In truth, my eyes were opened wide enough to see my life for what it really was in Montgomery. Welcome to Fallen Lake; welcome to the metaphor of your life, Andy Rosetti. Do you want to see what really goes on inside and around you on a daily basis? Do you want to know the wickedness of your own heart? How would you like to find out the root of your lukewarm temperature? What about those emotions you can't always understand or control? Oh, yeah, that's all here, too. Welcome to Fallen Lake; welcome to the spiritual realm of existence.

I like metaphors. I always have. After our long talk, Chantal and I spent the next night together, deciphering reality from illusion. I'd like to share our findings with you, since you've been along on this wild ride with me.

In Fallen Lake, we were tricked into believing that we were trapped on an island. In Montgomery, we were tricked into believing that we were trapped in our fears, failures, and weaknesses. The house we ran to for shelter, which seemed like such a beautiful safe haven at the time, represented the attractive and inviting sin we mistook for comfort daily in Montgomery.

In Fallen Lake, Bobby and Jon fought over Katherine. In Montgomery, Bobby and Jon were not really fighting over Katherine; Jon's interest lay only in bringing her out of darkness. The fight between Bobby and Jon in Fallen Lake represented the battle between the dark and light for Katherine's soul. In Fallen Lake, Katherine knew enough to flee from the house and the island. In doing so, she fled from temptation. What she did saved her from the angst that her other friends experienced. This was true also in Montgomery.

In Fallen Lake, all along Lisa had known the truth about the estate; she knew that they were inside Leslie's grandparents' mansion and that they were not on an island. She knew the darkness that haunted her own state of mind and the forces that were moving within the mansion. By remaining there, Lisa became susceptible to the sorrow waiting to encamp her. Why would anyone who knew the haunting truth of that place remain there? Lisa knew how to escape from the mansion's haunting dreams and occurrences. She knew the secret to protection, and she knew the way off of the island. Why did she remain in a state of such vulnerability? Notice that the darkness did not scare her, but the blood on the attic staircase put her under distress. In Fallen Lake, Lisa represented every person who had the head knowledge of God and knew the truth about the Blood of Christ but was unable to accept Christ as his or her savior. By staying many times at the mansion, which represented temptation leading to sin, Lisa had become enslaved in bondage.

In Montgomery, Lisa was bound just as tightly to the pain from her past. She let the loss of her parents keep her from loving and from allowing others to love her. God is love. By shunning love from her life, she was rejecting God's greatest commandment of all. To replace the love missing from her life she had turned to drugs and sex. She had hoped that the highs she obtained from both would fill the void of a loveless/Godless life. All it did was entrap her in bondage and keep her in darkness. As a result, she caved easily into the temptation of the world—everything that looked inviting, comforting, fulfilling, and appeasing. But it left her feeling violated—just as she felt in the mansion.

In both Montgomery and Fallen Lake, Chantal had been a source of light in Lisa's life. Lisa always kept a close watch on Chantal; she knew Chantal had exactly what she needed. How many people are in need of deliverance from demonic forces but write off their depression, anxiety, fear, rage, and anger as psychological disorders? I have come to learn that there are a lot of spiritually sick people in this world. For so long, I lived naïve to the spiritual realm. I was exactly where Satan wanted me to be. In Fallen Lake, Lisa kept urging me to find the truth. She did not want me to accept things at face value like she had. The longer I stayed in the mansion, the weaker I became to temptation. That was identical to my life in Montgomery.

In Fallen Lake, Chantal got upset when I did not flee from Leslie. In Montgomery, Chantal was upset when I did not flee from temptation. You see, the problem with me was that I walked around and called myself a Christian. It took Fallen Lake—a spiritual metaphor—to make me realize that my heart was not right with God. I had one foot in the church and one foot in the sinful world. Even though partying with drugs and alcohol was against my proclaimed morals, I partied with the best of them when Chantal was not around. I also flirted, charmed, and lied my way right up the social ladder of acceptance. The life I led around Chantal, my parents, and my church made me uncomfortable when I was with my friends. What I did with my friends made me uncomfortable around Chantal, my parents, and my church. I was caught between two lives—like how I was caught between Fallen Lake and Montgomery. I fit in nowhere. I had led myself to a dangerous place—accurately portrayed in Fallen Lake. There, I did not have God's protection because, in reality, I had not fully opened my heart to God.

In eighth grade, I "accepted" Jesus Christ as my Savior in order to impress the girl I liked. What I didn't realize back then was that God knew my heart and my motive. He knew the insincerity behind my profession of faith. Even though I believed in God, I had no desire to seek out His will for my life. I hadn't reflected enough on the Gospel to even comprehend what it meant to be a Christian. I had just wanted to date Chantal.

My insincerity of faith had prevented God from working in my heart. In turn, I worked my butt off trying to be everyone's idea of perfect. It was a daunting task. All the while, I couldn't understand the love Chantal exhibited to others. I didn't have it in me because I didn't really have Christ in my heart. I was deceived. I thought I was "saved" because I had said "The Sinners Prayer." I have learned that empty words do not equal a repentant heart. True repentance is more than remorse. True repentance means turning away from temptation and asking God to help you not to sin. It means depending upon Him to give you strength and grace to live a better life. It is understanding why Jesus died on the Cross and how it applies to modern-day life. We are saved by grace—God's unmerited love—through faith and not by good deeds. By playing "Christian," I had played with fire. I had done myself a complete disservice.

In Fallen Lake, Chantal had the ultimate protection; none of the demons could touch her without God's permission. In Montgomery, Chantal enters into spiritual warfare fully armed with promised victory because her Savior has victory over Satan and his kingdom. Chantal, unlike most teenagers, has a clutch advantage. Most people are oblivious to the spiritual realm and enter into battle unarmed and unaware that there is even a battle going on. In Fallen Lake, Chantal had rested safely in God's hand. He delivered her from evil and hid her in safety. Chantal said Psalm 27 had become real to her; the same was true in Montgomery. Through her trials with Jon, Alyssa, Cathy, and me, God preserved her, refined her, and kept her strong enough to refrain from damaging sin.

When I was in a coma, many people were praying for me. While most people had been praying for my physical health, Chantal had been praying for my spiritual health. She had prayed that God would wake me up to my need for Him. She had asked God to show me the lukewarm temperature of my heart. She had prayed for God to open my eyes to the truth of the compromising life I was living. She knew that God needed to break me before He could begin molding me into the best version of myself. Chantal left me in the potter's hands, and He broke me in a way that she never imagined possible. Fallen Lake was quite a vivid awakening, but it was exactly what I needed.

I used to walk around seeking people's acceptance, never wanting to offend anyone with my beliefs and focusing on life without much thought of eternity. Now, the thought of my loved ones suffering in Hell—day after day, without end—and being separated from God forever pains my heart deeply. It is enough to motivate me to share my story.

We have a God who knew us all intimately before the foundations of the Earth. He created us to have a relationship with Him; that is the purpose of life. How many people live life and miss the entire purpose of it? God, who loves us beyond measure—even though we make mistakes all the time—became human and dwelt among men to teach us how to live a fulfilling life. He came to die on the Cross and provide atonement for the sins of the world. Jesus paid our sin-debt of death so that we could live eternally in heaven with Him.

It took a near death experience for God to get my attention. I pray for my friends now on a daily basis. If it takes a persistent friend, a tragic accident, a natural disaster, or even my own death to wake them up to their need for Jesus Christ, I pray for it diligently. When I think about my freshmen year of high school and the revival that spread through my grade, it blows my mind. To think it all started with a bonfire on Saquish beach, a backslidden Christian named Courtney, and a burnout named Chris. God surely works in mysterious ways.

May you allow God to lead you to
the best path for your life;
May you realize that He created you for
a purpose that only you can fulfill;
May you believe with your whole heart
that you are special to Him.
—Andy

"For I know the plans I have for you," declares the LORD, "plans to prosper you and not to harm you, plans to give you hope and a future. Then you will call upon me and come and pray to me, and I will listen to you. You will seek me and find me when you seek me with all your heart." – Jeremiah 29:11-13

More Books by Stacy A. Padula

Gripped Part 1: The Truth We Never Told

In high school, Taylor Dunkin broke more records than any other athlete to step foot in Montgomery, Massachusetts. As a sophomore in college, he was ranked by ESPN as one of the NFL's top 100 prospects. However, his aspirations came to a jarring halt when a season-ending injury sent him spiraling into a dark world of pain, depression, and addiction.

One year later, Taylor is a person of interest in a highly confidential investigation headed by the Boston Police Department. He has entangled himself in a crime ring notorious for pushing drugs on local college campuses. Montgomery's hometown hero has fallen hard, and he's taking a lot of people down with him.

Luke Davids has become the middleman between Taylor and teens in Montgomery who want to buy drugs. Freshmen Cathy Kagelli, Chris Dunkin, and Jason Davids are just a few of the students at Montgomery Lake High who have fallen victim to the benzos and opiates supplied by Taylor and Luke.

When Taylor's youngest brother Marc discovers that Taylor is behind the copious amount of pills circulating around his high school, he sets off to not only reverse the damage Taylor has caused, but also save his lifelong role model from becoming a casualty of America's deadly opioid epidemic.

Gripped Part 2: Blindsided

Fourteen-year-old Chris Dunkin is known for being the life of the party and everyone's favorite friend. Despite his amicable nature, he carries around deep-seated pain from his childhood that he frequently numbs with alcohol and drugs.

After hosting a party, Chris awakes with a strange vibe running through his body and no recollection of the previous night. When he learns the horrifying truth of what his night entailed, the trajectory of his life is changed forever.

Gripped Part 3: The Fallout

Eighteen-year-old Marc Dunkin has received word from a detective that his oldest brother Taylor is a person of interest in a highly confidential case headed by the Boston Police Department.

They know Taylor's clean; they know he wants out of the game; and they want to help make that happen. However, their "help" will come at a cost—one that may put Taylor and his entire family in grave danger.

Twenty-three-year-old Taylor Dunkin is trying to get his life back in order after an opiate addiction wreaked havoc on his once promising athletic future. Getting clean was a difficult feat, but breaking free from the Bilotti crime ring will present an even greater challenge.

Gripped Part 4: Smoke & Mirrors

After spending her first month of high school grounded, Cathy Kagelli is finally allowed to socialize and uncover what her boyfriend, Jason Davids, has been up to without her. When Cathy realizes Jason has been experimenting with a variety of drugs, she devises a plan to save him from himself... but she just may lose herself in the process.

Meanwhile Taylor Dunkin finds himself playing a game with even higher stakes because his life, his reputation, and the safety of everyone he loves are all on the line. Taylor's two younger brothers, Jordan and Marc, have been at odds for years, but they are brought together to decipher the mysterious clues Taylor is leaving regarding his whereabouts. As secrets are revealed, the Dunkin boys' relationships will be changed forever. In Taylor's weakest moment, he made a deal with the devil, and now there is a reckoning. But who will pay the price?

Gripped Part 5: Taylor's Story

Taylor Dunkin is missing.

The last message Jordan Dunkin receives from Taylor leads him to Taylor's abandoned Jeep. Each of Taylor's family members holds a piece of the puzzle, and as the Dunkins begin putting the details together, they are awakened to the possibility they may never see Taylor again.

No one can find Missy Kent.

Missy's boyfriend Luke Davids last saw her dancing with their friends at a nightclub, but she hasn't responded to anyone's texts or calls for hours.

Everything is connected.

Taylor and Missy's friends are dangerously close to learning the truth, but their ignorance might be the only thing keeping them safe. Every clue is leading them closer to peril.

The fifth book in the Gripped series moves through details at a thrilling pace. Secrets are revealed and lives are at stake. Taylor, Missy, their friends, and their families must figure out who they can trust before it's too late.

Montgomery Lake High #1: The Right Person

Growing up in the shadow of two NFL-destined cousins, Chris Dunkin has high hopes for his own future in football. However, a drug addiction threatens to destroy everything he has worked hard to attain. When Chris meets Courtney Angeletti—the mayor's straightedge Christian daughter—he believes she could be the source of inspiration he needs to overcome his destructive lifestyle. Courtney, however, has other ideas.

The desire to rebel has been tugging on Courtney's heartstrings for some time, and Chris's "bad-boy" reputation draws her to him like a moth to a flame. After all, he is a central part of the most popular clique in her high school. Will Chris pull Courtney away from her faith or will Courtney inspire him to overcome his rebellious lifestyle?

Montgomery Lake High #2: When Darkness Tries to Hide

Students at Montgomery Lake High believe the ominous clouds and impending storm will only bring a temporary interruption to their regularly scheduled lives. However, when the tempest grows worse and a classmate's life hangs in the balance, students must pull together to support each other and seek help for their friend. As the lines between cliques dissolve, dark secrets are revealed and hearts are transformed.

Montgomery Lake High #3: The Aftermath

At age fifteen, Jason Davids appears to have it all: high grades, popular friends, a beautiful girlfriend, and nearly any worldly thing that promises enjoyment at his disposal. Despite this, there is a persistent emptiness inside his heart. After failing to fill the void with achievements, relationships, and illicit substances, Jason finds himself intrigued by Jessie: a rather quiet girl, who is the daughter of a local pastor. How is it possible that she stands for everything his lifestyle opposes yet possesses the one thing he has been searching for all along?

Montgomery Lake High #4: The Battle for Innocence

Jon Anderson and Chantal Kagelli are trying to live moral lives, but temptations are plaguing them in and out of school. Will they continue to be lights in their best friends' lives or will they get pulled into the darkness?

About the Author

Stacy A. Padula grew up in Pembroke, Massachusetts. She is the founder of Briley & Baxter Publications, the founder of South Shore College Consulting & Tutoring, a co-founder of BLE Pictures, and the author of fifteen books. She began writing her first book series, *Montgomery Lake High*, when she was a teenager because she saw a need for realistic Y.A. books that address topics such as substance abuse and bullying. Between 2010-2014 all five *Montgomery Lake High* books were published. In 2017, she began writing her second series, *Gripped*, which serves as both a prequel and sequel to her first series. *Gripped* parts 1-5 were published between 2019-2021. She is currently writing part 6. In 2019, she also wrote her first screenplay, an adaptation of her novel *The Aftermath*, and worked on writing a pilot for *Gripped*, which caught the attention of Hollywood producers. *Gripped* is currently being adapted for TV by Emmy award-winning producer Mark Blutman.

In 2020, Stacy began writing a third book series with NBA Coach Brett Gunning. Geared towards children ages three through eight, Stacy and Brett's *On The Right Path* series has been endorsed by Joel Osteen, Mike D'Antoni, and Kevin McHale as a series that belongs in every school, library, and household.

Stacy has been featured in Marquis Who's Who in America (2018-Present) for excellence in literature and education, Marquis Who's Who in the World (2018-Present), and Cambridge Who's Who for Young Professionals (2009). In 2018, she was awarded the Albert Nelson Lifetime Achievement Award, and in 2019, the International Association of Top Professionals (IAOTP of New York, NY) chose Stacy as its "Top Educational Consultant of the Year."

In 2020, she was named "Empowered Woman of the Year" by IAOTP and a "Social Impact Hero" by Authority Magazine for her support of animal rescues through her publishing company. She was also chosen to be on the cover of *T.I.P. Magazine*, an international business publication.

In June of 2021, Stacy was featured on the famous Reuters Building in Times Square as Empowered Woman of the Year. In 2022, she was named "Top Inspirational Author of the Year" and was honored at a gala at the Bellagio in Las Vegas. She was also broadcast for her award on the Planet Hollywood Jumbotron overlooking the Las Vegas Strip. Her novel *Gripped Part 5: Taylor's Story* won the Silver Award and *Gripped Part 1: The Truth We Never Told* won the Gold Award for "Best Teen Book" in the 2022 Readers' Choice Awards.

In 2023, Stacy was named "Top Global Impact Author of the Year" for her literary work on several continents, and she was honored at a gala at The Plaza in New York City. For this honor, Stacy was again featured on the cover of *T.I.P. Magazine*. She also accepted a position as a judge for the Scholastic Arts & Writing Awards, sponsored by Bloomberg Philanthropies, The New York Times, and Scholastic. She was named one of the *Top 50 Fearless Leaders for 2023*, alongside Mark Rivera from Billy Joel and former Miss Universe Michelle McClean. Later in 2023, she was named to her region's "40 Under 40." Lastly, her novel, *When Darkness Tries to Hide* won the gold award for "Best Teen Book" in the 2023 Readers' Choice Book Awards.

In 2024, Stacy was named "Woman of the Year" by The CIO TIMES and "Top International Social Impact Hero of the Year" by IAOTP. She was honored at a gala in Nashville, Tennessee. In addition, her publishing company was inducted into The Plymouth Business Hall of Fame for being the top publisher in its region, and her book, *The Aftermath* won the bronze award for "Best Teen Book" in the 2024 Readers' Choice Book Awards.

Stacy resides in Plymouth, Massachusetts with her husband Tim and her miniature dachshunds Baxter, Tony, and George. She attends New Hope Chapel and works daily with teenagers as a mentor and college counselor. She writes in loving memory of her first dachshund, Briley, who passed away in September 2024 at the incredible age of nineteen.

Connect with Us!

Gripped Book Series Instagram @gripped.book.series
Stacy's Instagram @author_stacypadula
Stacy's Twitter @TheGrippedBooks
Cathy's Instagram @ckagelli99
Chantal's Instagram @chantal_kagelli
Jason's Instagram @jds_on
Lisa's Instagram @lisa_ankerman99
Chris's Instagram @dunkin_85
Luke's Instagram @lukedavids97
Alyssa's Instagram @alyssa_kelly02
www.stacyapadula.com
www.brileybaxterbooks.com
www.highambition.org

Did You Enjoy MLH #5?

If you loved this book, would you leave a review on Amazon?